ENTANGLED HEARTS – VOLUME 2

YAHRAH

Published by Oliver Heber Books

OLIVER
HEBER
BOOKS

COPYRIGHT © Yahrah St.John

Published by Oliver-Heber Books

0 9 8 7 6 5 4 3 2 1

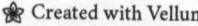 Created with Vellum

ENTANGLED HEARTS – VOLUME 2

YAHRAH

ENTANGLED HEARTS

VOLUME II

BY: Yahrah St. John

CHAPTER 1

*C*hynna James stared out into the dark night and wished she could go back in time. She wished she could go back and tell the man she'd fallen in love with the truth, but now it was too late. Tonight, Noah Hart had learned she'd been living a lie.

As one of the country's best-selling artists of all-time, Chynna's had never anticipated being rich and famous would not be all it's cracked up to be. She'd sold millions of records, had legions of fans and had all the money her hands and purse could hold, but she'd been unhappy until now.

A month ago, after a mishap with the press over a supposed affair with her married film co-star, she'd taken her life back. She'd called her identical twin, Kenya and they'd met at the Canyon Ranch Spa in Arizona. Chynna had come up with a daring scheme to switch places. Kenya would go back as Chynna allowing Chynna some time to find herself. In a week, they would switch back and no one would be the wiser. *If it only it had been that simple.*

Chynna walked over to the closet in the Hart's guest room, pulled Kenya's suitcase out and began pulling clothes off the hanger and throwing them inside.

Convincing her twin to take her place hadn't been easy, but Chynna had a persuasive argument. After years of living in her shadow, Kenya would finally see what it was like to walk a day in her shoes. Kenya had squawked at first, but eventually the prospect of acting in Chynna's first motion picture role had been the deciding factor. Her sister was a seasoned actress having acted on Broadway and was a regular on a critically acclaimed television dramedy series, but she hadn't made her big break yet. Dangling the carrot of working on a big budget movie had swung the tide in Chynna's favor and Kenya had agreed.

After a 24-hour marathon training session and hair color change, Chynna had sent Kenya back in her place and set about on a nature trek. *How could she have known that she would get lost and stumble onto the Golden Oaks Ranch and into Noah Hart's arms?* She sure hadn't and it certainly hadn't been love at first sight, though for Chynna perhaps it had been lust.

She walked over to the nearby dresser and threw some of the lingerie from it into the suitcase. Noah had been unlike any other man Chynna had ever met and she'd been smitten. Noah was a widower and breaking through his defenses had taken time, time she didn't have. So she'd kept asking Kenya for more time, a week here, another week there. She'd wanted, *no needed* to see if Noah was the real deal. He was. And she'd fallen for him hard.

Eventually, he'd let down his guard, long enough to let her in. Tonight had been their first date. He'd publicly taken her to his family's 35th anniversary party for their dude ranch and Chynna had been on top of the world.

She walked into the adjacent bathroom and began grabbing her toiletries on the marble countertop. She glanced at herself in the mirror and hated the person she'd become. She should have been honest with Noah from the start. He'd deserved to hear the truth from her, not from his brother Caleb.

Now he knew her name wasn't Kenya, but Chynna, *the* Chynna James, multi-platinum recording artist for R&K Records. And the look of betrayal she'd seen in his eyes at the discovery had broken her heart, which is why it was time for her to go. She had to leave the ranch before Noah asked her to.

"NOAH, you have to go after her!" Rylee Hart implored her older brother, Noah, after they'd just learned that the Kenya James who'd been staying at the Golden Oaks Ranch with their family the last few weeks was actually *Chynna James*, the famous pop singer. "Don't let things end like this."

Noah debated with himself for several moments. He still couldn't believe what had just happened. Kenya, the woman he was starting to fall for, was actually *Chynna James*? It didn't make any sense. Yet despite how upset he was at Chynna for lying to him, he needed answers. Why had she done it? Why had she lied to him and allowed him to believe she was someone else?

He decided to follow his sister's advice. "Excuse me," Noah nodded to his parents, Isaac and Madelyn Hart. He rolled his eyes at his wayward brother, Caleb, before rushing toward the main house. When he made it to the staircase, he took them two at a time until he reached the east wing where his sister and Kenya, *no, make that Chynna*, were staying.

He didn't knock on Chynna's bedroom door, instead he burst in. He found her sitting with a pile of clothes at her feet as she tried stuffing them unceremoniously into her suitcases, which he noticed looked rather expensive, probably designer no doubt. She'd changed out of the chiffon dress she'd been wearing and had changed into a t-shirt and jeans.

"Chynna!"

She jumped when she heard Noah use her real name. When she turned around, she wasn't staring at him as she'd done half an hour ago when the promise of *later* had seemed so thrilling, when he'd wanted nothing better than to remove the strapless chiffon dress she wore from her curvaceous body and take her to bed. He'd been ready to make Chynna the first woman he'd slept with since his late wife Maya's death. It was a big damn deal for him which why this was all *so* disconcerting. In a few short minutes, he'd gone from being horny as hell to having his entire world turned on its ear.

"I should've never stayed here," Chynna said, turning her back again to him to complete her task. "It was a mistake, and I'm going back to Canyon Ranch."

"So that's it?!" Noah roared. Just then, he heard a rumble of thunder in the distance, but he ignored it. "You're just going to leave? Don't you think I deserve some answers?"

"Is there really any use in me explaining?" Chynna asked, giving him a curt glance. "Will you believe anything I have to say now?"

"Well, I don't know Chynna, but perhaps you should give it a start," he said tersely.

Chynna threw into the suitcase one of the plaid shirts she'd purchased from the ranch general store and stood up to face him. He could see her warring with herself as if she didn't know where to start, so he helped her out. "Why don't you start from the beginning?"

. . .

4

CHYNNA WALKED over to the window and looked out at the patrons still mingling at the ranch's anniversary party. She was scared. She didn't know how Noah would react to hearing the reasons why she'd kept the truth from him or even if he would understand them. "I've been unhappy for quite some time with my singing career and when those pictures of me with Blake Cooper, a married actor I was working with, came out during rehearsals for my first movie, I bolted. I came here to Tucson—-to Canyon Ranch, to be with my sister, Kenya, to get away from the press who'd been dogging me."

She spun around to face him. "The two weeks at the spa with my twin were some of the happiest times I've had in years, and I didn't want to lose it. I remembered what it was like to be in control of my own life and destiny rather than doing what my manager, publicist and record label tells me to do. So *I* came up with the idea to switch places. Kenya would go to Los Angeles in my place, and I would stay at the spa and regroup, figure out how to claim my life and come back with a plan."

"It sounds plausible, but why would your sister agree to the arrangement?" Noah asked. It seemed like Chynna wasn't the only person unhappy with her life, because he couldn't imagine switching places with Caleb as a bullrider.

Chynna shrugged. She'd wondered that very same thing herself, but she'd been too selfish to really consider the reason Kenya had agreed to the arrangement. She'd just wanted out. "Perhaps she was unhappy as me? Anyway, we'd switched places before, and no one knew the difference, and it wasn't going to harm anyone. It was only supposed to be for a week, and we'd switch back."

Another roar of thunder echoed, and Noah sensed

rain was upon them. He could only imagine their guests would be running for cover and his family could probably use his help to tear down the party, but he couldn't leave, not now. He *needed* to hear more.

"On my first day alone at the spa, I took a drive and decided to go hiking to another location Kenya had mentioned. On my way back, I was accosted by these cattle." She saw a reluctant smile cross Noah's features at the memory of their first encounter. "They caused me to hit a fence and when I woke up ..." she paused, looking into his deep dark-brown eyes, "I saw one of *the* most handsome men I'd ever met."

Noah raised an eyebrow. He highly doubted that to be true. In her line of work, Chynna was surrounded by beautiful people. *Why should she be intrigued by a simple rancher like me?*

Chynna recognized the self-doubt in Noah's eyes, but continued her story. "The first moment I met you, Noah, I felt something, and I was curious to see where it went. There wasn't an ulterior motive, I just felt something real and genuine for the first time in years." Her voice choked but she continued on, "And the more you pushed me away, the more I became intrigued. Especially when you challenged me that I wasn't good enough or too bourgeoisie to stay, so after my first week passed, I asked Kenya to stay on—and well, Kenya was having the time of her life playing me." Chynna laughed derisively. "Seems she's managed a love connection with the one man I'd always been trying to catch. How's that for irony?"

She glanced in Noah's direction, but he wasn't laughing in the slightest. In fact, she could feel the rage inside him seething on a slow boil.

"Why didn't you tell me the truth, Chynna?" Seconds later, he heard the tap of rain against the window-pane. Noah looked toward the window! *Dammit!* He needed to know the answer to his question, but there was a lot to be done outside, and his family would need his help.

"Go!" Chynna sighed. "They'll need you."

Noah stared at Chynna long and hard for several long moments. He hated to end this conversation without having the answers he so desperately needed, but he had a duty to attend to all his guests. "We'll finish this conversation later."

"I don't know, perhaps I should—"

But Chynna didn't get the words out, because Noah interrupted her. "Promise me, you'll stay until we've talked." His dark eyes burned into hers, and as much as Chynna wanted to get out of Dodge, she owed Noah, heck the entire Hart family, an explanation and at the very least a thank you for the hospitality. "Okay."

"We'll talk later," Noah said, and soon he was out the door, leaving Chynna to wonder when he came back if there would be anything left between them.

AFTER AN HOUR and Noah hadn't returned, Chynna went downstairs to see if there was anything she could do. There was a lot of commotion going on. Party staff had brought the food and decorations in from the anniversary celebration outside and the house was bustling with people and activity.

Chynna eventually found Madelyn and Rylee in the kitchen trying to organize the efforts. "Is there anything I can do?" she asked, looking at both women.

"Roll up your sleeves and help us start packing up this food," Madelyn replied.

Chynna noticed that Madelyn didn't quite look her in the eye, but she understood. She'd lied to them all, except Rylee. Rylee gave her a half-smile as they put the food in the containers and double refrigerators throughout the kitchen.

"We'll have to take some of this food to our guests for the inconvenience," Madelyn said.

"Will that even be possible?" Rylee pushed the blinds aside to glance out the window. "It's raining cats and dogs out there."

"Let's just make due for now," her mother said.

The Hart men, Noah, Caleb and Isaac, eventually returned to the main house shortly thereafter and came barreling through the back door by the kitchen. Noah's and Isaac's suit and Caleb's fresh clothes were soaking wet.

Madelyn pointed at her men. "Don't take another step." She placed her hand up to stop them. "Take off those clothes right there in the mud room."

"Maddie—" Isaac started to enter the kitchen, but his wife held her hand up.

"Don't you Maddie me," she said. "I don't want you tracking mud throughout the house, so just strip right there."

Caleb laughed. "But Mama, we do have guests," he said, looking directly at Chynna, "or should I say a celebrity? We wouldn't want to damage her delicate sensibilities."

"You hush, now, Caleb," Madelyn replied, "or I'll give you something to laugh about."

"Yes, ma'am." Caleb was quiet after the admonishment and began removing his clothes like his father and brother.

Chynna noticed that Noah remained quiet throughout the exchange and did as his mother asked. She tried to hide her curiosity by focusing on boxing up the decorations, but her eyes couldn't resist wandering over to Noah as he removed his tuxedo jacket and shirt, followed by his trousers. She swallowed when she saw him standing in nothing but his boxers and undershirt.

She quickly glanced away but not before she caught Rylee smiling mischievously at her.

"Go on up the backstairs." Madelyn nodded her head in the direction of the staircase. "I wouldn't want you to give the staff a surprise. I'll have your clothes laundered." She walked over and put the soiled clothes in a basket from the mud room.

The men did as they were told until eventually it was just Madelyn, Rylee and Chynna in the room. When they'd completed putting all the food and decorations away, Madelyn turned to Chynna and asked, "So you're a singer? Who would have ever guessed?"

"I was trying my best to hide it," Chynna responded.

"Sounds like there's a story to tell."

Chynna nodded.

"Well, I'm dying to hear it."

"We all are," Caleb said, sauntering into the room. His father was right behind him, followed by Noah. They'd each showered and changed. Isaac was wearing pajamas and a robe while Caleb and Noah had changed into T-shirts and sweats.

Chynna wasn't ready to tell her story to the entire family, especially not before she and Noah had time to talk. But she'd been put on the spot, so she had no choice. "I'm sorry for lying to you all," she began, glancing around the room, "Really, I am. And I'll be leaving tomorrow and be on my way."

"Well, I doubt you're going anywhere tomorrow, sweetheart," Caleb replied with a slight twang as he took a seat at the kitchen island where the women stood. "The roads are washed out. We heard on the radio that the highway patrol was out closing the roads because rain is expected the next couple of days. Flash flooding is expected, so you might be here a few more days."

"Are you saying I'm stuck here?"

"Looks like it," Caleb said, chuckling. He looked over at his brother, who was standing quietly by the doorway with his hands folded across his chest. Caleb didn't understand why Noah didn't just forget the lies and take the woman in his arms and damn it all to hell. He supposed that's why he and Noah were so different. He was a man of action.

"Well then, it's settled," Madelyn said, giving her a friendly smile. "Chynna will be our houseguest for a while longer." Madelyn looked at Noah, and said, "Isn't that great?"Noah didn't answer. Instead he turned on his heel and walked out of the room.

"Excuse me," Chynna said, rushing after Noah. She caught him in the foyer and grabbed his arm. He glanced down at her hand on his arm, and she instantly moved it away.

"Can we talk?" she implored.

"It's late, Chynna," Noah said. It was well after one am, and he was exhausted, not only physically but mentally. He'd been on such a high tonight having her as his date; he'd thought nothing could touch him, nothing *except lies.*

"But ...," Chynna paused. "But, we haven't finished talking. You asked me why I lied. And—"

He cut her off. "Does it really matter?" While helping friends and guests to safety, taking down the anniversary party decorations and buttoning down the ranch, Noah realized he didn't really know anything about Chynna. He'd just been caught up in the moment of meeting this beautiful woman who'd been unlike any other woman he'd encountered. And now he knew why. She was so out of his league and his stratosphere. He thought it was better that he distance

10

himself now before he fell harder for this beguiling woman.

"Yes, it does. At least to me," Chynna replied, but she noticed his nose wrinkle. "But not to you anymore? Is it so easy to turn your feelings on and off, Noah Hart? If so, you're a lot colder than any man I've ever met in LA. You have a good night." She pushed past him, her full breasts lightly touching his arm as she stomped up the stairs.

Noah watched Chynna run upstairs wanting to go after her, but for some reason he was paralyzed with fear. Fear of what? The unknown? He wasn't sure. But he did know that his heart ached watching her go.

"Wow, you really handled that one well, bro," a masculine voice said from behind him.

Noah spun around to find Caleb leaning against the doorway with a beer in his hand.

"What do you know?" Noah snatched the beer from him, took a swig and handed it back before walking across the hall to the living room.

Caleb followed him as he had done a million times before when they were kids. "I know that I haven't seen that look in your eye in a long time."

Noah glared at him. "What look?"

"The look I saw when I first got here. The starry-eyed look you used to have with Maya."

Noah rolled his eyes and stormed over to the French doors to watch the rain come down.

"You don't know what you're talking about, Caleb."

"Oh, yes I do," Caleb said, rushing over to Noah and spinning him around. "That woman," he said, pointing upward to the ceiling with his beer bottle, "is the first woman to pierce," he poked Noah's chest with his index finger, "that heart of yours in a long time, and it's got you running scared."

"You have no idea what you're talking about."

"Like hell, I don't!" Caleb swigged his beer. "She's got fire and spirit and is easy on the eyes too."

Noah's eyes narrowed into harsh glints at his younger brother. "Watch it."

Caleb smiled. "And you're jealous. Why? Because you want her for yourself, Noah. Well, guess what, bro? You can have her. All you have to do is go up there and take her. Make her yours. You know you want to."

"You've fallen off those bulls one too many times, and your head isn't screwed on straight, Caleb."

"Are you seriously going to deny that you weren't going to take her to bed tonight?" Caleb laughed, "In that hot dress?"

Noah took a dangerous step toward him, but Caleb side-stepped his brother and moved farther away in the room. "You're in denial, my friend. And I am going to enjoy having a first class seat seeing you eat crow." Caleb bowed his head and then seconds later he was gone, leaving Noah in the living room alone.

Alone with his thoughts. Alone to wonder why he hadn't taken Caleb's advice and gone upstairs and made Chynna his like he'd wanted to do earlier. *Am I using the lie Chynna told me to keep her at arm's length and avoid letting go of the past?*

CHYNNA AWOKE the next morning feeling surly. She'd tossed and turned the night before, all in a feeble attempt to forget the betrayed look on Noah's face last night. The look that told her that her lie could have cost her the one man she'd cared for in years—the one man who wasn't using her as a meal ticket to get ahead in his career.

She'd finally awoken, showered and changed into a velour jumpsuit and twisted her hair into an impromptu updo. She wasn't eager to face the Hart fam-

12

ily, but there was no avoiding them seeing that she was stuck on the ranch for the next few days. The rain was still pelting the windows even now. How was she going to deal with being cooped up with Noah without an escape?

Several minutes later, she found the Hart family was already seated in the formal dining room, eating breakfast. Isaac and Madelyn sat at opposite heads of the table. Noah must have done his best to ensure he was not seated beside her, because the only seat remaining was next to Caleb.

"Good morning, Chynna," Madelyn said, speaking first. It was odd to hear her *real* name being used, but also comforting. She could be herself now. No more lies.

When Chynna hadn't moved from the doorway, Caleb patted the seat beside him. "Come sit."

"Good morning, everyone." She gave a half-smile at Rylee before walking over to Caleb, who made a production out of jumping up out of his seat and pulling her chair out for her.

"Thank you," Chynna said, glancing across the table at Noah. She could feel the tension coming off Noah, even though he hadn't looked up at her. He seemed intent on cutting his pancakes into small bites.

Once she was seated, Caleb wasted no time with pleasantries and took the liberty of pouring her a glass of coffee from the carafe. "So, what's it like being a superstar and all?"

"Caleb," Rylee sighed. As much as she loved him, sometimes her younger brother had no tact; he didn't know when *not* to rile things up. No, instead, he just jumped in, head first as always. She'd hoped they could table the matter of Chynna's celebrity and have a normal breakfast at least until dinner. No such luck.

"It's okay," Chynna said, nodding in Rylee's direction. Chynna took a quick sip of her coffee, which she drank black. This part she didn't mind. She knew people were curious about what it was like to walk a day in her shoes. And now her twin was doing just that, yet Chynna suspected Kenya was finding out that all that glitters isn't gold. "Usually, it's kind of fun," she said, answering Caleb's question. "There's the adoration, the glory, the awards."

"And I'm sure lots of money," Caleb said.

"Yes, Caleb, the money is great." She smiled as she reached for a carton of yogurt from the center of the table. "And the perks aren't bad either. I get free clothes and handbags and the best tables at restaurants and clubs." She sunk her spoon into the creamy mixture and ate.

"But then?" Madelyn asked the question that not many people would think to ask. "What comes after the money and fame?"

"Then there's the paparazzi," Chynna said, rolling her eyes. "And up until now, I hadn't given them anything to chew about."

Rylee shot Chynna an incredulous look, which prompted Chynna to clarify, "Okay, they may have played me up as a party girl, but that's nothing compared to the last few weeks. The vultures smell fresh meat, and it's been horrific since that picture was taken with my movie co-star. They follow me everywhere. They stalk me outside of my house waiting in their dark SUVs and chase my car down the street. They are trying to catch me when I'm unaware or looking distraught so they can sell the photo and have a big payday. I'd always wanted to be famous, but never infamous."

"That's terrible," Rylee said, sympathizing. "It makes sense why you used your sister's identity."

"So the press has no idea where you are?" Isaac asked, sipping his coffee.

Chynna nodded as she finished her yogurt and put down her spoon. Again, she looked at Noah. He was finally taking an interest in her account of what had transpired.

"Wait a sec," Caleb said. "The press said you've been back in LA for weeks, been spotted with your new man, a Lucas somebody, even had a concert. So, if the press thinks you're in LA ..." His voice trailed off as he tried to put the pieces together.

Chynna pointed her finger. "You got it. My twin and I traded places."

"Traded places?" Madelyn put her fork down. "How?"

"We're identical," Chynna explained. "Most people forget, which in this instance played to our advantage. When Kenya and I met up at Canyon Ranch for some R&R a couple of weeks ago, she reminded me that I'd forgotten who I was and why it was that I enjoyed singing and creating music to begin with." Chynna paused and took a sip of coffee. "You see, I started out wanting to be unique ... you know, different from the other R&B singers."

"Your first album was amazing." Rylee couldn't help gushing as she tore into her Western omelet. "I played it all the time."

"Sure did," Caleb snorted. "Drove us all mad."

"But the more successful I became, the more stress and pressure I received to conform to the masses. And after Mama died ...," Chynna's voice choked and she stopped mid-sentence. Even now after three years had passed, talking about her mother still hurt.

"When did she pass?" Madelyn asked softly. "It must have been hard for you to lose your mother, especially so young."

Chynna nodded, fighting back the tears on her eyelids. "It was a few years ago, and I took it pretty hard. I distanced myself from Kenya and allowed myself to get carried away by the partying and carousing. Pretty soon I started doing what people told me to do to keep up with the ever-changing music scene rather than be the artist *I* wanted to be."

"And now you're trying to find yourself?" Noah asked for the first time, acknowledging her presence.

Chynna glanced up at him through heavy eyelids. His eyes were unfathomable, and she couldn't read them. "Something like that," she said, shrugging. "I guess I'm trying to remember the Chynna I used to be ... before Mama passed ... before I let all the fame and money suck me in."

"Sounds like a smart plan if you ask me," Isaac Hart replied and looked at his son. "Sometimes you have to take a few steps back to reflect on the past before you can move forward with your future."

Chynna understood exactly what he meant. "Kenya and I talked for hours at the spa, and that's when it came to me. Kenya is such a great actress and a phenomenal singer—always has been, and she could easily imitate me." She shrugged. "So I thought 'Wouldn't it be cool if I just took a little break and she went off for a week to be me?'"

"And she agreed to leave her life and go in your place?" Rylee asked.

Chynna smiled. "I think Kenya has always wondered what it would be like to be me. And now she's had a chance to see the glitz and the glamour."

"In the midst of this media whirlwind?" Madelyn asked. "You are giving her some pretty big shoes to fill."

"She can do it," Chynna said, smiling broadly. "Kenya is an amazing actress and a gifted singer herself.

She's been in dozens of Broadway shows like *RENT* and *MEMPHIS*."

Rylee giggled. "I loved those shows."

"Are you addicted to pop culture?" Caleb ragged on his big sister. "Sounds like we need to get you some other hobbies."

Rylee rolled her eyes at him.

"I knew Kenya could handle herself for a couple of weeks. Plus, she'll get to walk a mile in my shoes."

"Wonder how she'll feel after a couple of weeks," Caleb muttered under his breath, "with the press nipping at her heels?"

"I've wondered that myself and thanks to Mother Nature, I'll have to wait and see."

TENSION COURSED through Noah's veins. Being this close to Chynna was driving him crazy. Everywhere he went, she was there. If he went to the kitchen, she was in there with his mother trying to be helpful with lunch or dinner, even though she'd probably never used a skillet a day in her life. If he went to the study, she was with his father, Isaac, playing gin rummy as they listened to jazz on vinyl, his dad's favorite pastime.

He'd finally ventured out in the rain to the stables to check on the animals even though he had staff to do it, just to get away from her. Apparently, he wasn't the only person seeking the attention of the animals. Rylee too was in the stables wearing a rain slicker.

"What are you doing out here?" she asked when he came through the stable doors. She'd delivered a new philly in the wee hours of the morning and had come by to check in on her. She'd found her nursing under her mare.

"Just needed some air," he said, standing in the doorway and watching the rain come down.

"You mean you needed to get away from Chynna?"

Noah turned around. "You can tell?"

"Uh, yeah," Rylee said, laughing. "We all can. Whenever the two of you are in the room together, you can cut the tension in the air with a knife. Don't you think you need to talk to her?"

"I already did."

"Liar."

Noah shrugged. "I've heard enough. She wanted to get away from her life and how does she go about it? She puts her sister, her twin for Christ's sake, in harm's way, all in an effort not to deal with her own issues."

"Really?" Rylee put her hands on her hips and stared at Noah incredulously. "You of all people are going to stand there and judge her, when you yourself have been hiding behind Maya's death for the last two years? You're one to talk, Noah Hart."

"I lost my wife! That's not the same thing."

"And she lost her mother," Rylee countered. "Didn't you hear her story? She spiraled after her mother's death too. Maybe she lost her way for a bit. Does that sound familiar? Perhaps you could show her some of the compassion that we've shown you instead of judging her so harshly."

"It's easy for you to say, Rylee. She didn't lie to you. You knew the truth. She confided in you. You're not so innocent here, little sis." Rylee lowered her head at his accusation. "While she keeps me, the man she supposedly 'has feelings for'" he said, using his fingers to make air quotation marks, "was in the dark. So how about you give me some time to process the truth *you* already knew." Seconds later, Noah was walking out of the stables.

. . .

CHYNNA EMERGED from the stall with a rack in her hands. She'd been helping Rylee check on the foal in an effort to get out of the house too. Her eyes were wistful as she watched Noah's retreating form through the sheets of rain that were coming down. "He really hates me, doesn't he?"

"He doesn't hate you." Rylee turned around to face her. "He's just angry with the circumstances, but I know my brother." She walked toward Chynna and grasped both her hands. "He's a good man; he'll come around, just give him time."

That's what Chynna was afraid of. Because time was something she had a short quantity of. Kenya would want her life back, which meant Chynna was going to have to go back home and face the music.

CHAPTER 2

*K*enya James awoke with a start to the sun streaming through the blinds and in Lucas Kingston's bed. *How the hell had she gotten here?*

Oh yes, she'd let her sister Chynna talk her into switching places with her. Kenya had returned to Los Angeles in Chynna's place and she'd resumed not only her concert tour, but acting in her first movie. Kenya hadn't thought she could do it, but somehow she'd convinced all the people who swarmed about Chynna's everyday life from her manager Deacon Clark to her publicist Fiona to her assistant Penelope that she was really Chynna. No one had given her grief except one, Eli Ross. Part owner of R&K Records, Eli couldn't understand the personality shift and had been watching Kenya closely. And then there was the other half of R&K Records, Lucas.

Kenya glanced down at Lucas in the bed beside her. Last night, they'd gone to bed together. *What had she been thinking?* Kenya smiled. She hadn't been. She'd been going off instinct, primal instinct.

For the last three weeks since she'd been imitating Chynna, she and Lucas had been circling each other like cats in heat. The attraction between the two of them had been instant from the moment he'd been waiting for her inside the limo when he'd *personally* come to Arizona to bring 'Chynna' back to LA. Kenya had tried to resist the pull even though they'd shared more than one passionate kiss on occasion, but Lucas had been so damn persistent.

Last night, he'd shown up at her doorstep unannounced, determined to take her out for dinner and – one thing had let to another and now here she was in his bed. She tried to crawl out of bed, but Lucas' arm was sprawled across her middle and as soon as she moved, Lucas stirred beside her. In the cold light of day, Kenya couldn't regret the night she'd spent making love with Lucas. It had been everything her previous sexual encounters had lacked. Exciting. Passionate. Thrilling.

But Kenya *did* realize that it might not have been the wisest decision to go to bed with him given she was imitating her sister. Lucas had no idea that she was Chynna's twin. He thought she was the superstar singer he'd always thought was a spoiled princess but had suddenly transformed. He had no idea who she truly was because she hadn't had the courage to tell him the truth. And she wanted to, but she was caught between a rock and a hard place. She couldn't be honest with Lucas without revealing Chynna's secret.

Slowly, Kenya slid out of Lucas's grasp and nearly fell on the floor, but she managed to catch herself before waking Lucas up. Kenya rose and looked down at his sleeping form. He was sleeping so soundly that she wished she could snuggle back up next to him and forget the world existed, but she couldn't.

Kenya picked up her clothes strewn across Lucas's bedroom and one of her shoes. Glancing around her back, she saw that Lucas hadn't awoken, and she quickly went to dress in his spare bathroom. Kenya looked at her reflection in the mirror. Her hair was tousled, her skin bright and her lips swollen from Lucas's kisses. Why couldn't life be easy?

She'd promised Chynna that she would trade places with her and allow her sister the time to figure out her life. The funny thing was, Kenya had discovered something about herself. She'd learned that she liked the limelight just as much as Chynna and, more importantly, that she was just as talented.

Kenya opened the bathroom door and tiptoed out of his bedroom without Lucas hearing a sound. She found her other shoe in the hall and put it and the other on her feet. She hated creeping out in the wee hours of the morning and taking the walk of shame, but there was no way around it. She couldn't go back on her word. If she told Lucas the truth, it would blow Chynna's world apart. She had to stay true to the course despite how much it might hurt her in the end, despite the fact that she was starting to fall in love with Lucas Kingston. Opening the front door, Kenya walked out into the morning sun.

LUCAS AWOKE half an hour later and reached across for Chynna only to find the bed empty beside him. He sat up and looked around the room and then to the bathroom door, but didn't hear a sound. Had she really snuck out of his bed like a thief in the night?

Lucas threw off the covers in a huff and walked buck naked into his bathroom. He walked into his ceramic tiled shower and turned on the taps. He stepped under the pulsating hot water and let it rain on him. He thought they'd shared some pretty damn good sex. He'd made sure he'd satisfied her several times throughout the course of the night both inside her and when he used his mouth and tongue to bring her to a finger-curling scream of an orgasm. He'd dreamt of making love to her again this morning and burying himself deep within her tight sheath. He'd been surprised just how tight she'd been, but when she'd clenched her muscles around him, he'd become unglued, groaning and moaning her name as his hands tugged at her hair. It had been the best sex he'd ever had.

Lucas splashed water over his face to wake himself out of his daze, but he felt no more alert and couldn't understand what could have happened to change Kenya from the sexual being he'd made love to back into the scared woman he'd been courting for weeks. He was determined to find out. Lucas wasn't going to allow Chynna's fear to get in the way of something great happening between them. Last night had just been the start.

HAVING DRIVEN to Lucas's in his Ferrari, Kenya had the unpleasant task of calling Deacon early that morning to ask him to come and get her from Lucas's place. She felt like such an idiot that she didn't even have enough money for a taxi. Kenya guessed that's what happened when you got used to everyone taking care of everything for you: You forget how to take care of yourself.

"Hop in," Deacon said after he'd arrived twenty minutes later in a sporty Mercedes-Benz.

She must have looked a sight wearing last night's dress with her smudged makeup and tousled hair. She was sure it was clear what she'd done last night, but much to Kenya's surprise, Deacon remained silent for the entire ride to her mansion. She thought she'd escape a lecture, but then he turned off the engine when they arrived and followed her inside.

"Why don't I make some coffee," Deacon said as Kenya made her way up the circular staircase.

Kenya paused midstride and glanced over her shoulder. She rolled her eyes upward.

"I'll meet you in the kitchen," Deacon said, without waiting for her answer.

Kenya tried to take as long as she possibly could, showering and washing her hair, but eventually she had to depart the steaming room and face the music. Or in this case, Deacon's disapproval. After blow-drying hair straight, she dressed in a tank top and yoga pants and met Deacon downstairs in Chynna's big eat-in, yet modern kitchen.

Kenya liked the stainless steel appliances, but didn't care for the cherrywood cabinets and granite counter-tops. She would have preferred an all-white country kitchen.

"Can I pour you a cup?" Deacon asked as Kenya approached the table.

"Would love some." Kenya pulled out the seat adjacent to him and plopped down.

Deacon slid over her mug and Kenya reached for creamer nearby, but he frowned. "You drink your coffee black."

"Usually," Kenya said, but she was dying for a sugary concoction for once. She was tired of Chynna's eating habits and wanted to indulge.

"You don't need the extra calories and it's a bad habit," Deacon said, smacking her hand away, "Like other things."

Kenya rolled her eyes. "You obviously have something to say, so why don't you spit it out."

"Chynna, I know that you do things your own way," Deacon began, "and it's one of things I both love and hate about you."

Kenya narrowed her eyes.

"But even you must see that a sexual relationship with Lucas will only end in heartbreak."

"Deacon, I don't need a lecture from you."

"Well apparently you do," Deacon said. "I'd hoped it was just some harmless flirting, but my fears were confirmed today. You don't need this kind of drama. You finally have things on track with your music and the movie. Getting involved with Lucas will only distract you."

"Is that your only fear: That I won't remain focused?"

"It has happened in the past, not to mention that Lucas is not the commitment kind."

"So what?" Kenya huffed. "What if all I want is a fling?"

"Bullshit, Chynna," Deacon said. "I know you. You may put on fronts for other people, but remember I know you and you love with your whole heart. Just like you did with that idiot Lamar. I don't want you to get your heart broken again."

"I won't allow that to happen," Kenya said. Why? Because there wouldn't be time. Any day now, she would be going back to New York, and Chynna would come back to Los Angeles, and any relationship Kenya had with Lucas would come to an end.

"Famous last words," Deacon said.

Kenya smiled broadly. "Well, don't get your panties in a twist ole' boy," she said, reaching across the table and patting Deacon's hand, "because I agree with you."

"You do?"

Kenya grinned. "Yes. I was just giving you shit. As much as I may have enjoyed last night, it's in the past, and it won't happen again."

"Are you sure about that?" Deacon said. "Because if I know Lucas, he will not take no for answer."

"In this case, he'll have to," Kenya said firmly. "Last night was a one-time thing." And she was really going to have to play Chynna's spoiled princess role even better than Chynna herself, because that's the only way she would convince Lucas to give up. She would have to show him Chynna hadn't truly changed, show him that the old Chynna had never left and it was all an act. She was going to have turn on the DIVA.

THE REST of her morning consisted of running lines with Penelope for the next day's shooting on the movie and some voice lessons with a coach that Carter Wright had insisted she work with. Kenya was surprised at how comfortable she was getting at having so many people around her, but there was something to be said for alone time.

"Do, ra, me, fa, so, la, te, do," she sang the musical scale notes.

"You're used to belting out songs onstage," Carter told her during the last scene they'd shot, "but I need you to be more controlled in your singing for those quiet moments."

Kenya was well aware of those quiet moments. She was used to pacing herself during her run on Broadway, but because she was playing Chynna, who sang at stadiums, she'd had to act differently. When she was finished with the coach, she drank nearly an entire Evian before sitting down with Deacon and Fiona, who'd just arrived.

"So, there's obviously something going on," Kenya said, "or you both wouldn't be here."

"There's a club opening tonight by an A-list celebrity," Fiona said, looking up from her iPad. "Everyone is going to be there. You need to make an appearance with Lucas."

Kenya's eyes instantly darted to Deacon. She saw the look of disdain on his face. He'd warned her about keeping her distance from him and she was sure was not happy about this latest development. "Chynna James never misses a LA club opening," Fiona replied before Kenya could jump in. "And you and Lucas need to be seen together. The paps are talking about how you guys gave them the shaft last night at Spago. Couldn't you have at least allowed them a few shots?"

Kenya looked down. "We just wanted some time alone."

"Time alone for what?" Penelope asked, smiling.

"Mind your business," Kenya snapped, and immediately her shy assistant returned to sorting the piles of fan mail that came to Chynna's house everyday.

"C'mon, Chynna," Fiona said. "We all agreed to this weeks ago, and you promised you would live up to your end of the bargain."

That she has, thought Kenya. She just hadn't planned on going to bed with the man. But that wasn't Fiona's fault; she was doing her job and cleaning up Chynna's image by showing her off with a single, available man. Kenya was just going to have to suck up her emotional baggage and view it as a job. But that was hard to do.

Throughout the day, as she'd run lines or sang scales, her mind had drifted to Lucas's sexy grin, those chiseled abs, that rock-hard behind that she couldn't resist slapping in bed. Or was it his intellect and the fact they could discuss any topic from religion to politics to movies to music. Lord, she was falling hard for this charismatic man.

"Did you hear what I said?" Fiona's voice burst through her reverie.

"No, I'm sorry. Can you repeat it?"

"Are you going to give me a hard time, or can I contact Lucas and arrange the date?"

Kenya rose and waved her hand in the air. "Do what needs to be done." Somehow, someway she would find a way to mask her growing feelings for the music mogul.

LATER THAT EVENING, in true Chynna fashion she had on spike-studded peeptoe stilettos and a black leather and mesh dress with a cutout at the side. The dress barely reached her thigh and with the four-inch heels, she was all legs. When she came down the stairs, Deacon gave her a whistle.

Deacon didn't look too bad either. He'd changed into a dark gray suit with a silver tie. Fiona had donned an emerald-green cowl dress that draped from her shoulders by a single rhinestone-studded chain. With her striking red hair, Fiona was a knockout.

"Fiona, you look amazing," Kenya commented.

Fiona blushed. "This old thing. It's nothing."

"Bullshit," Penelope said quietly from the corner. "She agonized over what to buy all day yesterday."

Kenya couldn't help but chuckle. Penelope might be quiet, but she was observant. "So where's Lucas?" she asked breathlessly. She was ready to get it over with. She hadn't seen him since she'd rushed out of his apartment earlier that day, and she could only imagine he was less than pleased with her.

"I'm right here," a deep masculine voice said from behind their group, and Kenya's stomach lurched.

When the group parted to allow Lucas to enter their circle, he wasn't wearing the frown Kenya imagined he would—he was smiling. Later, she would find out it was just for show.

"Lucas," Kenya said, reining in her nerves even though her heart was going pitter-patter at his nearness. She had to remind herself: DIVA. DIVA.

"Chynna, you ready to give the paparazzi what they want?"

"That is why we're going through this charade," Kenya said haughtily and without a glance as Lucas headed toward the door.

Deacon glanced at Fiona and Penelope and said, "This is going to be a long night."

LUCAS STARED at Chynna from across the limo seat. If looks could kill, she would be dead instantly. He was angry that she'd walked out on him without a word or an explanation. He hadn't considered their night together a hook-up. He'd hoped it would be a mutually satisfying relationship for both of them, until ... until it ended, which it inevitably would.

He didn't do long-term relationships. Never had. Growing up in South Central, he'd dated, but he hadn't wanted to get too close for fear one of the girls would try to trap him and he'd never leave. Then, as he'd gotten older and more successful, the same scenario had been true. Wannabe singers and groupies would swarm him, desperate for their big break, and if he got too close, BAM, they'd trap him. Trap him into fatherhood or marriage. Or both. Neither of which were in the cards for him.

He'd seen his mother go from man-to-man having baby after baby until she was fifty, with five kids by different fathers. He'd been the only boy of five, and his sisters had become victims of their environment and had started the cycle all over again. That's why he'd had to get out or his family would suck him in. After he'd become a millionaire, he'd bought his mother a house and helped support his siblings when he could, but it seemed like they perpetually needed a handout. So he kept his distance, visiting only at holidays and the occasional birthday. It was a solitary life sometimes, but

Lucas didn't want the drama that family sometimes could bring.

When the car stopped, Lucas realized he hadn't spoken a word to Chynna the entire ride. Even Deacon and Fiona looked nervous sitting across from him with Chynna.

"Everything okay?" Deacon asked, noticing the dark expression on Lucas's face.

"Everything's fine." Lucas blinked several times, reminding himself that he couldn't change where he came from, only how he ended up.

"Smiles then." Fiona made a grin motion with her hands, "The press is going to be looking at both of you," she said, turning to Chynna at her side, "for a crack underneath the surface, and if they find out, they'll pounce."

"No worries, Fiona," Kenya said. "We've got this. Don't we Lucas?" She stared him dead in the eye, and he could see her challenging him to say otherwise, but he didn't rise to the occasion.

"That's right," Lucas said, and seconds later he was jumping out of the car.

AS SOON AS she exited the vehicle, Lucas's arm encircled her waist on the red carpet for the paparazzi waiting at the new club. Cameras and light bulbs flashed in front of Kenya's face as she smiled and posed for the press.

"Lucas, are you missing the single life?" one reporter asked.

"Of course not." Lucas flashed a kilowatt smile. "How could I be when I have a woman as beautiful and talented as this one?" He leaned down and brushed his lips across Kenya's.

The paparazzi went wild, pointing even more cameras at them, so much so that the bouncers had to usher them both inside to allow for the other guests and celebrities to arrive for the event.

"You weren't lying when you said those people are vultures," Kenya said, smoothing down her dress. As much as she might have been easing into Chynna's life, she doubted she could ever get used to the skimpy clothing her twin was supposed to wear.

Kenya and Lucas walked into the darkened club with the flashing lights and were greeted not only by a packed house but by Eli, Lucas's business partner.

"Eli." Lucas leaned over and gave Eli a one arm hug.

Eli hugged Lucas back, all the while giving Chynna the once-over—"I like," he said to Fiona, as if she Chynna exist. "Did the press get some pictures?"

Lucas rolled his eyes. "Tons. I think we've given them something to chew on for a while. Where you at?"

"I have a VIP table for us," Eli said. "Follow me."

Most of the evening was spent schmoozing with other celebrities, drinking champagne, and nibbling on appetizers, but the true entertainment came when the stage became dark, and then six women appeared in the spotlight complete with bustier and thigh-high fishnet stockings.

"What's going on?" Kenya asked, looking around the table.

"Didn't we tell you?" Eli grinned. "It's a burlesque show."

"I can see that," Kenya said. "What type of club is this?"

"Oh, a little of this, a little of that. This is LA," Eli said. "Do you have a problem with it?" But before she could answer, he said, "If I recall, you liked these sorts of shows, said it gave you material for your concerts."

Kenya stared at Eli blankly. *Does Chynna really think that?* She wondered as she stared at the woman gyrating on stage and manipulating scarves, whips and chains.

"Maybe you should get up there and show them how it's done," Eli taunted.

Kenya couldn't figure out his problem, but Eli was definitely in a mood tonight. She'd never really cared for him, but he was behaving like even more of an ass.

"Not while she's my woman," Lucas said, pulling Kenya protectively toward him for the benefit of their table, which had grown from their small group to include several of Lucas's business associates and two actors from Chynna's new film. "The only person she's going to be giving a peep show to is me. Isn't that right, darling?"

Kenya plastered a smile on her face, even though she was smacking his hand away underneath the table. "Only for you, babe."

"I need a stronger drink than this champagne," Eli said, suddenly getting up from the table. "Can I get you something, Lucas?"

"Yeah, man, a Scotch would be great," Lucas said. He turned to Kenya. "Chynna, what would you like?"

Kenya wasn't much of a drinker because she couldn't hold her liquor. "Nothing for me."

"Oh, c'mon, Chynna." Eli eyed her suspiciously. "You've never been known to turn down a drink."

"Maybe that's the problem," Kenya replied. "I'd just prefer to keep my wits about me. Thank you, but if you insist, I'll have just a virgin strawberry daiquiri, please."

Eli stared at her long and hard for a moment, but rather than argue with her like he always did, he moved away toward the crowd of people standing at the bar.

ELI STARED through the crowd back at Chynna. Lamar was right. Something wasn't quite right about Chynna.

She hadn't been the same since she'd gotten back. It was almost like she was a different woman. The moment the words came to his mind, Eli knew they had to be true. Chynna wasn't the same person because the woman imitating his recording artist was her twin! *Why didn't I figure this out before?*

Chynna has a twin, an actress ... named ... Eli racked his mind trying to remember her name, but he just couldn't put his finger on it. It was the name of a country. *How can I prove she is an impostor?* If he told Lucas, or anyone for that matter, they'd think he'd lost his marbles. Why would a Multi-Platinum artist like Chynna leave her lush lifestyle and trade places with her sister? *And if her twin is playing Chynna, where is the real thing? Where has the little minx gone?*

Eli was going to find out. He already had a private investigator watching Chynna's every move, but that was before he knew the score. Now, he had something to give him. The investigator could start with the twin first and work his way from there. Chynna and her sister were not as smart as him, and he would figure out what they were up to before they ruined everything. And he knew exactly what he was going to do to pay that bitch, her twin, back. She'd been giving him hell since the day he'd arrived, but he had something for her. Oh, yes, she was about to be taught a lesson that she couldn't mess with Eli Ross.

When the bartender asked what he wanted to order, Eli said his usual Hennessey and Coke and for Lucas he ordered a Scotch, but he also ordered a strawberry daiquiri for Miss High and Mighty, heavy on the rum. The sweetness of the drink would mask the liquor and finally her inhibitions would come tumbling down.

* * *

KENYA SLURPED up her second daiquiri for the night. "Hmmm, this is really good, Eli," she said. She'd never recalled the drink tasting quite this good before.

Eli smiled. "Oh, that bartender really knows what he's doing." Eli had ensured it by tipping the bartender a hundred bucks to keep his mouth shut and keep the liquor flowing.

"Well, I want another," Kenya said, tossing her hair back flirtatiously. She'd never felt so giddy and loose before. "Let's dance." She bumped her hips against Lucas in the booth.

"I'm really not ...," Lucas began, but before he could finish, Kenya was nearly crawling over him to get out of the booth. "Okay, okay." Lucas looked at Eli suspiciously for a minute, just as Kenya tugged his arm and led him on the dance floor for a fast song.

Kat DeLuna's song "Whine Up"—one of Kenya's favorite dance songs—came on. Soon Kenya had her hands on her hips and was shaking her bottom in front of Lucas. She noticed his eyes perk up at her seductive dance. So she slid her fingers through her hair and wound her hips more to the pop song. She could see Lucas trying to hold back, but she was having none of it. She didn't know what had come over her, but she wanted him something fierce like she had last night. She turned until her backside was against his crotch and melded her body against his. She leaned her head back, allowing her hair to dangle against his face. At first, Lucas resisted, but eventually he gave in and pulled her closer to him. As he wound his body with hers, Kenya could feel his erection growing underneath her. She rubbed provocatively and shamelessly against him, until he eventually spun her around.

"As much I love this dirty dance of yours," Lucas said, looking into her eyes, "you're drunk."

"No, I'm not. All I had were daiquiris."

"Spiked daiquiris," Lucas replied, and he had a feeling he knew was behind it. He looked through the crowd to the table where Eli sat, smiling like a Cheshire cat.

"C'mon." Lucas grabbed her by the arm and walked her unceremoniously off the dance floor.

When they returned to the table, Lucas announced they were going home.

"Why?" Eli asked, laughing. "We're all having fun. Aren't we?" He looked at Deacon and several other celebrities at their table.

Deacon gave Kenya a cursory glance and noticed her slouched posture against Lucas's arm. "I think our girl should be calling it a night. We do have that big show in Vegas day after tomorrow, and we can't have Chynna tying one on and spending all day tomorrow in bed instead of rehearsing."

"But Chynna has always known how to hold her liquor," Eli emphasized. "What's changed?"

Kenya looked into Eli's beady eyes, and for the first time saw what she hadn't the entire night. *Does Eli know? Does he know I'm not Chynna?* She struggled to compose herself, although the liquor had already had its desired effect, which is exactly what Eli wanted. He wanted her off her game. "I, I didn't eat anything today." She gave a half-smile to the table. "The liquor went to my head."

"Sure kid. Have a good night, everybody." Lucas inclined his head and led Kenya away from the table and out of the club.

LUCAS GLANCED down at Chynna's sleeping form in the limo on the way back to her mansion. Eli was right about one thing: Chynna could usually hold her liquor. But this new Chynna, since she'd come back from the spa, had been different. She was poised and in control. Until last night. Last night, she'd finally let go and gave into the passion that had been building between them for weeks.

And he'd let go too. For the first time in his life, he'd felt a connection other than sex when he was intimate with a woman. And this morning when he'd woken up to find her gone, he'd been angry not just because he wanted to take her back to bed, but because he'd actually started enjoying her company and hadn't wanted it to end.

Chynna stirred on his lap and Lucas stroked her honey-blond hair. When she'd flung her hair back on him on the dance floor and ground that tight little butt of hers against his penis, he'd wanted to turn her around and bury himself deep inside her welcoming body. But Chynna wasn't herself tonight. He was sure Eli had spiked her daiquiri just to be spiteful. Chynna gave him grief and Eli had wanted to teach her a lesson. Lucas hated that side of his friend. He had ever since they were kids. It wasn't enough that Eli was the biggest or the baddest. He could be mean just because he could, but never to Lucas. Lucas was the only person that Eli would listen to, but that didn't mean he could behave any kind of way, and Lucas was going to have a word with him in the morning.

The limo came to a stop, and Chynna peered up at him through mascara-coated lashes. "Are you coming inside?"

Lucas could see the green specks in her hazel eyes, and his groin swelled at the implication. Lucas rolled his eyes upward and prayed for strength.

Lucky for Lucas, Chynna didn't stay awake for long and promptly conked back out. He slipped his hands under her and carried her from the limo into the house and up the stairs to her bedroom.

Her bedroom was everything he'd imagined it to be —glitz and glamour. Yet that wasn't the only Chynna he knew. There was more to her than she portrayed to the world.

Lucas laid her gently onto her king-size bed. She stirred only for a moment as he slid the strappy sandals she'd been wearing from her slender feet and tossed them to the floor. He debated with himself for about half a second before deciding to undress her. He looked around the room for a nightshirt. Finding nothing, he searched her dresser drawers and found an oversized NYU T-shirt that looked like it had seen better days. Now came the task of taking the skintight dress she'd been wearing off her delectable body without wanting to ravish her.

He managed the task, but had a raging hard-on for his efforts. She wasn't wearing a bra underneath the slip of a dress, which only increased his discomfort. Her round, curvy breasts and delicious brown nipples were bare, and she was wearing a scrap of fabric that barely covered the triangle between her thighs.

Lucas swore under his breath. He so desperately wanted to take her nipples in his mouth and tease them into hard buds, but he couldn't take advantage. Chynna had had too much to drink, and he wanted her stone-cold sober when he made love to her again. Quickly, he slipped the T-shirt over her head, pulled the covers back then slid them over her. But instead of going home, he kicked off his loafers and joined her on the bed.

He told himself that he was staying over to keep an eye on her and make sure no one took advantage, because he didn't want to think too long or too hard about the real reason he was staying over because if he did, he'd have to acknowledge something he wasn't yet ready to admit to himself.

CHAPTER 3

Chynna's phone stopped working, and she didn't realize it until the second evening of the flash flood. She'd been so caught up in Noah and the ranch's anniversary party and then later the flood and getting through to Noah that she hadn't even thought of Kenya. They hadn't spoken in days, and when she finally tried Kenya, her cell didn't work.

On the one hand, Chynna felt terrible for being so selfish and only thinking of herself. Kenya had to be worrying about her and wondering when Chynna planned on returning. But on the other hand, the additional time without interruptions might give her time to get through to Noah. Rylee seemed to think that there was still a chance for her and Noah, and Chynna needed to find out. She would make one last ditch effort to get through to him. No matter what he said, she was going to have to pull out all the stops or risk losing him forever.

LATER, when dinner was over and the older Harts had retired to bed, Rylee, Noah, Caleb and Chynna sat around downstairs in the living room chatting as the winds and rain beat against the windowpane.

Although Noah was civil to her, Chynna hadn't been able to break through the ice he'd started forming again around his heart. So Chynna used the one weapon in her repertoire. While Noah and Caleb sat chatting on the sofa and Rylee played on her iPad, Chynna went over to the piano and began playing a new love song she'd been writing since her arrival in Tucson.

She closed her eyes and sang softly with the piano as her only accompaniment. Eventually, she was so caught up in the music and the lyrics that she didn't realize all conversation had ceased and she had an audience watching her.

When she opened her eyes, Rylee and Caleb were staring at her, open-mouthed, but it was Noah who was studying her. His eyes searched her face, reaching into her thoughts, and instantly she knew that he knew the song was about him.

"That was amazing," Rylee whispered breathlessly.

"You have a gift," Noah echoed his sister's sentiment.

"You're telling me," Caleb said as he lounged back in the recliner. "I still can't believe I have Chynna James sitting in my living room serenading me. Wait until I tell the fellas at the rodeo."

Chynna spun around to face Caleb, and said, "You can't tell anyone about this." Her eyes flashed with a gentle but firm warning. "If you do, word will leak and the ranch will be surrounded by cameras, SUVs, helicopters and more. You have no idea the can of worms you'd be opening on your family."

"I don't want the family or our guests disturbed by the ruckus. They've been through enough with this storm," Noah replied, "so Caleb will be keeping his mouth shut. Isn't that right, Caleb?"

Chynna was surprised Noah's words had a degree of warmth and concern, though not directed at her.

"Of course," Caleb said, offering a forgiving smile. "I was merely saying that none of the fellas will believe me when I tell them."

"I'll give you one," she said, holding up her index finger, "One photo as proof." She watched a slow grin spread across Caleb's face, and she added, "When I leave." He frowned.

"Fine," Caleb said as he rose from the lounger and headed for the door. "I'm going to go find some action."

"Better not be with any of our guests," Noah yelled to Caleb's retreating figure.

After he left, Rylee stifled a yawn with the back of her hand. "I'm exhausted. I was up early this morning delivering that filly, and I'm pooped." She rose from the sofa. "I'm heading up to bed. You ready, Chynna?" she asked, looking down at her houseguest.

Chynna shook her head. "Oh, no, you go on. I'm not tired yet. Guess I'm still accustomed to the late nights on the road."

Rylee looked at her brother, but could sense that he was sticking around to have a word with Chynna. She wasn't sure what was about to go down, but figured she'd make a hasty exit. "Alright then, I'll see you both in the morning."

Once the door closed behind Rylee, Noah wasted no time walking over to Chynna at the piano.

"Well, it's clear you have something to say to me, Noah," Chynna said, "so why don't you just get it off your chest."

"Was that song about me?" Noah asked, placing his beer bottle on the piano.

She glanced up at him. "What makes you think that?"

"Are we really going to play these games, Chynna?"

Her brow crinkled. "Fine. The song was about me and you. I write whatever I'm feeling at the time."

"Did you mean what you said about wishing you'd had more trust in me? Do you wish you'd told me the truth from the start and not waited for Caleb to rat you out?"

Chynna let out a heavy sigh as she rose from the piano bench and moved closer to him. "Of course I do," she replied. "But I can't change the past, and you're just going to have to accept me as I am, flaws and all."

He stared into her eyes and then down at her mouth before turning his back on her.

"Jesus, Noah," Chynna spoke with a fragile shaky voice. "I, I can't read you from one minute to the next. You have me on a merry-go-round. One minute you hate me and want to strangle me ... and the next ..."

Her voice trailed off, but Noah was intrigued and spun around. "And the next, what?"

"And the next, I think you want to kiss me," Chynna answered honestly, looking him in the eye. She wasn't backing down. Not this time. "Make love to me."

Noah licked his lips in agitation. "M-make love to you?" He repeated her sentiment back in a husky whisper.

Chynna could read men and knew that Noah was trying his best to act that he was unaffected by her, but she knew that wasn't the case. It was time to make her move.

NOAH'S ANGER had already gone, and he didn't know why he was still holding on to it. Maybe he was using it as a shield to keep Chynna at bay? One thing was for sure, when she moved closer to him and one of her hands encircled his neck and pulled him toward her warm, parting lips, his resolve evaporated. The look in Chynna's eyes told him that she was a tiger, and he was her prey.

He wanted her to kiss him. She melded her lips to his and his tongue found hers. He stroked, cajoled, teased and caressed until he was lost.

Then Chynna broke the kiss. When she looked at him her pupils were dilated and glassy with desire. She didn't say another word; she just grasped one of his large hands in hers and led him out of the living room and toward the spiral staircase.

"Chynna ..." Noah stopped her on the stairs even though ripples of excitement coursed through him.

The imploring look she gave him told Noah there was no more time for words, just action.

They climbed the stairs in silence, and when they reached the second floor, Chynna started for her room on the east wing, but Noah pulled her toward the west wing, his wing. He was the only occupant of it, and they would have no interruptions.

Chynna smiled a mischievous grin and allowed him to lead her to his bedroom. When they arrived, Noah turned on the lamp on his nightstand, giving the room a soft hue of light. Chynna was so beautiful; he didn't want to miss a minute of seeing every inch of her in all her glory.

Chynna was still standing at the door, but only long enough for Noah to hear the click of the lock on his bedroom door as she slipped off her flats. He smiled knowingly. *Smart girl.*

He swung her into the circle of his arms and pressed his lips against hers while his hands moved everywhere. There were no tentative touches, just hot, drugging kisses. She kissed him back long and hard and he answered her with all the pent-up frustration he'd been harboring for the last couple of weeks since she'd gotten on the ranch.

"Make love to me, Noah," Chynna murmured against his lips.

"I'm going to do just that," Noah said.

Need surged through Noah. He wanted to explore every inch, every curve of Chynna's body—make her moan and beg for him to bury himself inside her, and he would have all night to do it. Slowly, he pulled away and stared into her hazel eyes. As the rain battered the roof overhead, Noah knew that deep down, he'd always known that he would make love to this woman.

"Chynna," Noah said with a shaky breath, and he searched her face for some sign that she wanted to stop. Seeing none, he reached down and began unbuttoning her plaid shirt. When it fell open, Noah could see her nipples through the lacy number she wore underneath and he swore. "Have I told you you're one of the sexiest women I've ever met?"

"No," Chynna said, smiling, "but it's nice to hear."

"I mean every word," Noah said as he removed the shirt from her body, and it fell to the floor.

But Chynna wasn't going to be an inactive participant. She slid her hands up under his T-shirt and hiked it up over his head in one fluid motion and tossed it aside. Before he could stop her, she made easy time of his jeans buckle and zipper, and soon his jeans were hitting the floor along with its predecessor. Noah appreciated her enthusiasm and stepped out of his jeans, leaving him standing only in his boxer briefs.

But if she thought she was in control, she had another thought coming. He reached for her, crushing her to him, and took her mouth with an intensity that surprised him. His tongue delved inside her mouth, while his hands worked at the waistband of her jeans. Unsnapping them, he slid them down her curvy behind without breaking the sweetness of their kiss. And when he did, it was only long enough to lift her off her feet, lay her on his bed, and remove the denim from her long legs.

With her honey-blond hair fanned out on his bed and wearing next to nothing, the magnitude of the moment hit Noah. He was going to be intimate with a woman other than Maya. And for the first time, he didn't feel guilty about moving on with his life. It was time, and he was going to begin the moment with Chynna.

CHYNNA GLANCED up at Noah and for a fraction of a second, she could see him *thinking* and wondered if he'd changed his mind. She wouldn't let him. She lifted her arms, clasped them around his neck, and pulled him down with her onto the bed, and he fell into her mass of arms and legs. His thighs and calves were chiseled and strong—a clear indication of a rancher's hard work, and it looked good on Noah.

Making love with him would be different from the sex she'd had with other men over the last few years. Tonight she was going to close her eyes and give in to every gnawing need she'd held inside for this man. She moved her hands up and down his body, stroking his lean back and moving her hands over his tight butt like she'd imagined in her dreams. Except this time, it was real. This time, she could feel his response as she rubbed herself seductively against him.

"Easy love," Noah said, shifting slightly until he was on his side facing her. "I want to take my time and savor you, touch you, kiss you."

No one had ever said those words to her. Usually, men she slept with wanted to hit it and quit it, but

Noah—he was different, and she'd known it from the start. It's why she hadn't been in a hurry to go back to her life, but eventually she would. But for tonight, she would shut thoughts from her mind and just *be with him*.

"Don't take too long," Chynna said.

He responded by reaching over to pull her in his arms and kiss her long, hard and deeply. Her lips parted, and she drank in the sweetness of his kiss and the mastery he showed by making her moan with desire. She heard the snap of her bra and felt the tenderness of his touch as he spun her over to her stomach. He pulled back her hair to place feather-light kisses and light flicks of his tongue on the back of her neck, shoulders and spine. It was completely sensuous, and pleasure radiated from every pore of her being.

His hands moved down the length of her back to massage her buttocks, the back of her thighs, knees and calves as he searched for her pleasure points which were particularly sensitive spots for her and when he found them, low groans escaped Chynna's lips.

"Oh, yes ..."

"You like that," he murmured, glancing up at her. But Chynna was powerless to answer, because her senses were spinning.

Noah made a path upward long enough to divest her of her panties, discard them and kiss her butt cheeks. Chynna sighed with pleasure. When his body finally slid upward and brushed past her, Chynna felt his burgeoning erection in his shorts, and she reached behind her to take him in his hands, but Noah was having none of it and pushed her hand away.

"There will be time for me later," he said. He was on a mission, and when he flipped her back over, his mouth found one of her breasts that had been aching for his touch. He fondled one mound with one hand while his mouth ravished the other breast. The tugging sensation of his mouth drove her wild. He teased one nipple, laving it with his tongue, circling the tight bud over and over again until Chynna thought she might die if he didn't do the same to the other. As if reading her mind, he glanced up devilishly and paid her other breasts equal attention and fervor, but this time he added another element by sliding his hands down her body to the triangle between her legs that was dewy with moisture, and he parted the folds with his fingers to delve inside.

Chynna nearly jumped off the bed at his intimate embrace. Not because she didn't want it, but because she didn't just want his fingers there, she wanted *him*, *all of him*. She wanted to feel him deep inside her. She was dying for it, aching for it, but Noah was going to make her wait.

His finger slid in and out of her wet heat while his tongue played with her nipples. Chynna began to squirm under his deft caresses.

"Please, Noah."

"Please, what?" he asked, lifting his head to look up at her.

"I need you."

"Soon, babe," Noah said, and before Chynna could react, he'd pushed himself down to her waist, propped both of her legs over his shoulder and ducked his head between her thighs.

Chynna felt his tongue seconds later at the entry to her womanhood. He blew air at her slightly, and she shivered just as his tongue entered her. Her hips involuntarily arched off the bed as she gave herself over to the master of his tongue. He dove inside and out, in and out with deliberate precision.

"Oh, God!" Chynna's hips arched upward, eager for more of his intimate embrace.

"Yes, babe." Noah tongued her with delight. "Come for me."

He slid his tongue and finger inside her simultaneously, up, down, in and out, side to side. He circled her clitoris with such delicious torture that Chynna finally became unglued. She released all her inhibitions and cried out, "Noah!"

Noah lowered her legs from his shoulders and moved upward to brush Chynna's tousled hair from her face. "Was that good?"

"Can't you tell?" she asked with heavy-lidded eyes.

A free and easy smile came across his lips. "Yes, and it's not over." He spun away from her and off the bed. When he returned a few minutes later and lowered himself back on the bed, Chynna heard the crackle of foil and turned to watch Noah slide a condom on his large shaft. As much as she'd enjoyed his earlier ministration, Chynna was ready for the main event.

Noah poised himself above her, and Chynna opened her eyes to see him gazing at her intensely—it was an honest, open and passionate expression. The look told her just how much she and this moment meant to him without him saying a word. It was a look of promise and perhaps the possibility of a future, but Chynna was too afraid to think about that now. Her response was to close her eyes and wrap her legs around him, letting him know it was okay. Noah answered by slowly pushing forward into her wet opening.

Chynna accepted all he had to offer. Having him inside her body felt like home, and she could feel her inner muscles expand and contract as he thrust forward, filling her completely.

CHYNNA WAS SO HOT, so slick, so wet as Noah slid himself with one push inside her that he thought he might lose himself right then and there. It had been a long time since he'd been with a woman, but Chynna wasn't just any woman. As he began thrusting inside her, his fingers danced over her skin, skimmed her body and her hips.

Her eyes were slightly closed, but he could see the waves of ecstasy as they washed over her face, and he wanted Chynna to ride the wave with him. He reached between her legs and worked his fingers between the folds of her womanhood as he pumped inside her and her eyes flew open. This time, he held her gaze, and as he plunged in and out, she whimpered noises of pleasure.

He bent to her breast—suckling, nibbling and pulling at it with his lips while his hands moved from inside her to cup her buttocks so he could thrust even deeper, pounding into her. Chynna clung to him, and her nails scratched his forearms with each fierce thrust. Noah was lost. He was caught up in a whirlwind that only Chynna could calm.

She screamed first and began bucking underneath him, which triggered his orgasm and wave after wave of delight coursed though him. He shouted and collapsed on top of her. Thank God he had the entire west wing to himself or he would have woken up the entire house.

"That was incredible," Noah said quietly as he slid onto his side as to not crush Chynna.

He glanced over at Chynna and sweat gleamed on her bosom.

Chynna slid to her side and stroked his cheek. "That was amazing," she said. "Wanna do it again?

THE NAGGING SOUND of a cricket awoke Chynna from her sleep the following morning rather than the

49

blinding sun which had been up for some time. She found herself in Noah's bed alone, but the occupant was still in the room.

Noah was standing bare-chested, wearing a pair of jeans and staring out the window with a cup of coffee in his hands. The fact that he hadn't seen her awake gave Chynna time to not only watch him but reflect on what had taken place between them the night before.

They'd made love not once, not twice, but three times last night. They'd been insatiable for each other and had made love until nearly dawn. Flashbacks of last night's lovemaking came to her mind. Chynna smiled when she remembered straddling Noah and riding him as wave after wave of sheer delight consumed her. Chynna blushed when he'd surprised her by flipping her first on her knees so he could make love to her from behind. She shuddered when she thought about how he grasped both her arms behind her as he thrust inside her and how she'd come twice during the encounter.

As if sensing she was awake, Noah spun around from the window to face her. Had he been thinking about their incredible night of lovemaking? Or worse was he regretting their night of passion?

"Good morning, sleepyhead," he said, taking a sip of coffee that he liked to drink black. "Would you care for a cup?" he asked, pointing to his cup.

"Would love some," Chynna said, smiling as she sat up and brought the sheet up to her bosom with her. She watched his eyebrow raise at the action. "But how did you get it?"

"I went downstairs and got some and brought a carafe up." He motioned to a tray sitting on the nightstand beside Chynna.

"Well, then I'll have some," Chynna said, flipping her legs over the side of the bed. She glanced around the room, looking for something to wear, but didn't see her clothes.

Noah walked over to the bed and retrieved the plaid shirt he'd been wearing last night and handed it to Chynna. "Is this better?" he asked, holding out the garment.

"Yes." Chynna let the sheet lower, revealing her naked body to Noah's gaze, but quickly slipped his shirt on and began buttoning it. She didn't know why she was self-conscious in the morning light, considering everything they'd done last night, or rather, this morning.

"Was anyone up?" Chynna inquired.

Noah smiled mischievously. "Why do you ask?"

Rather than answer, she poured herself a cup of coffee from the carafe on the tray. Finally she said, "Well, from the looks of it, it's rather late, and your family was probably wondering what happened when both of us didn't show up to breakfast."

"I'm sure they've figured it out."

"Noah!" Chynna chided, turning to glare it him.

"What?" Noah shrugged. "We're both adults and what we choose to do behind closed doors is none of their business."

"It's not that simple when you live in your parents' home." She sipped her coffee.

"Of course it is," Noah said. "Maya and I had no problem keeping our private life private."

As soon as he said his wife's name aloud, an uncomfortable silence took over the room. Chynna wondered if he'd been thinking about her as he stood at the window staring out over the ranch.

Noah placed his coffee cup on the nightstand and scooted next to her on the bed. He took one of her hands in his and said, "I'm sorry I brought her up." Sensing her uneasiness, he added, "I wasn't thinking about her while we were together, Chynna, if that's what you're thinking." He caressed her cheek softly with hands roughened from his labor on the ranch, and with an index finger he turned her head to face him. "There were no ghosts in my bed last night. It was just me and you."

Chynna smiled and inwardly gave a sigh of relief. "Okay."

"How about some breakfast?" he asked. "I think cook left a breakfast casserole downstairs warming on the stove."

"I need a shower first." She rose to her feet and started peeling his shirt from her body, and this time, unabashed by her nakedness, she turned around and said, "Are you joining me?"

"Hell, yeah," Noah said, jumping off the bed. He pulled a new condom off the three-pack and rushed into the bathroom.

THEY MADE it downstairs for a late breakfast an half an hour later after Noah had made sweet love to Chynna in the shower. He'd joined her under the taps and had soaped and washed every part of her body. Then he'd backed her up against the wall, wrapped her long legs around his waist and joined them as one. The friction of her soapy body rubbing all over him as he thrust into her wet body had been intoxicating. He'd buried himself deep inside, and Chynna had matched his every thrust until eventually they'd both cried out their release.

Now they were walking into the kitchen hand-in-hand, prepared to face the onslaught of questions, but the only person sitting in the room was Caleb with a cereal bowl.

He glanced up when he heard their footsteps, took

one look at them and said, "Well, well, well. Now I know why I thought I felt the earth move last night." He chuckled.

Chynna blushed furiously at his side, but Noah walked over and popped Caleb across the head. "Watch your tongue."

"Hey, what was that for?" Caleb asked, moving away from another one of Noah's blows. "I speak the truth."

"Keep your truths to yourself," Noah said, pulling out Chynna's chair so she could sit across from Caleb. "Where's everyone anyway?"

"Now that the rain has lifted, Mama and Daddy are out surveying the damage and soothing the guests ruffled feathers."

"I should be out there," Noah said, walking over to the stove and removing the foil off the breakfast casserole. Cook knew it was one of his favorites, with eggs, potatoes, sausage, onions and cheese. He sliced two generous pieces and put them on a nearby plate on the counter. Then he popped them into the microwave.

"Appears to me like you were otherwise occupied," Caleb said as he sunk his spoon into his cereal and took a mouthful.

"Did anyone ever explain tact to you?" Chynna had finally spoken up.

Caleb laughed and glanced her way. "Glad to see you aren't afraid to talk."

Chynna smiled broadly. *If only he knew.* Until recently, she'd had that very same problem, but not anymore. Speaking of her life, she owed Kenya a long overdue call. "Will you excuse me for a moment?" She rose from the table. "Now that the weather has improved, I need to call my sister."

"What about breakfast?" Noah asked, holding up the plate of casserole he'd just heated.

"Just put it on a plate for me," Chynna said. "I'll be

right back." Seconds later, she was walking out of the kitchen leaving Noah and Caleb alone.

Noah put one slice on another plate and took the other with him along with a glass from the cupboard and sat next to Caleb at the table. He reached for the pitcher of orange juice his brother had left sitting out on the counter and poured himself a glass.

"Well?" Caleb's brow rose a bit.

"Well, what?" Noah asked, annoyed.

"How was it?" Caleb nudged him with his shoulder. "You know, your first time with Chynna."

"I am *not* talking about this with *you*," Noah said, digging into his casserole and taking a bite.

"Who else are you going to talk to about it?" Caleb asked, "Dad, Rylee? I don't think so. Just spill the beans. I'm dying to know."

Noah sighed. "Fine." There was no use in him acting like he and Chynna had not just become intimate when it was written all over their faces, not to mention that they'd come into the room holding hands after they'd been polite for the last two days since the anniversary party. "All I'll tell you is that last night was hot."

Caleb's forehead crinkled. "Better than you and Maya?" He was surprised, given that Maya was the love of Noah's life. Or was she?

"Not better, just different," Noah said introspectively. It had been what he'd been milling over at the window when he'd woken up that morning. He knew Chynna thought he was thinking of Maya, but he hadn't been, not in that way. He'd been thinking about how different both women were and how he'd fallen for each of them. And fall he had. Even though he'd only known Chynna for a short time, she'd awoken something in him—a part he'd thought had died with Maya. She was spirited and feisty, and she'd challenged him, pushing through the barriers he had around his heart, but now he wondered where that left them. Chynna led a different life from him, and he wasn't sure where he fit in.

"What's wrong?" Caleb watched Noah intently. He could see his brother was musing on something, but what he didn't know.

Noah turned and glanced at the door Chynna had gone through minutes ago. "I was just wondering what's next."

"That's the problem with you, Noah; you always want to know what's around the corner. Don't think so much, and just enjoy the moment."

Noah desperately wished he could do that, but something deep down told him that his time with Chynna could be short-lived.

CHAPTER 4

*K*enya woke that morning with a splitting headache. She searched her memory for what happened and then she remembered the daiquiris, the delicious concoctions that Eli kept handing her all night. She had a flash of the dirty dance she'd given Lucas on the dance floor, and Kenya closed her eyes, hoping it was a dream, but she knew it wasn't.

She turned her face into the pillow to block out the memory, and that's when she felt someone behind her and noticed a masculine arm draped around her middle. Then she saw a tuxedo jacket draped across the nearby chaise. *Oh, Lord, did I pick up someone and take them home?* It would be completely out of character for her, but then again, so was getting drunk. She prided herself on never losing control like she had last night. Damn that Eli! He was the reason she was in bed with some stranger.

Was there anyway she could extricate herself without them realizing she had left? Kenya tried to move away without disturbing the arm, but when she did, he pulled her more snugly against his middle, against his hard middle. OMG, like most men, the man had a hard-on that morning, but it did feel like he had on pants. Was he going to expect her to put out as she'd probably done last night? She glanced down to see if she was wearing any clothing, and she was. She was wearing her NYU T-shirt that she'd had since her college days. Had he put her in it? Before or after they'd had sex?

Kenya was embarrassed beyond belief, but didn't know what to say when the masculine voice behind her said, "Good morning."

Her heart began racing a mile a minute when she heard the owner of that smooth baritone voice. *It's Lucas!* She'd spent the night again with Lucas after she'd promised to stay away from him. Had she said anything to him in the throes of her drunkenness? Had she given herself away?

Slowly, she turned around to face Lucas. "Good morning," she said tentatively.

"How are you feeling?" he asked. "You were pretty wasted last night."

"Was I really? Did I say anything crazy?" *Please say I didn't. Please.*

He gave her an irresistibly devastating grin. "No, though I did enjoy your dirty dance, was even dreaming about it. It was very arousing."

That much was obvious, and Kenya pushed against his chest until she was a few inches away from him. "Lucas, you're incorrigible!"

"No, what I am is horny," Lucas said, "but I refused to take advantage of a woman under the influence."

Kenya's brow furrowed. "Are you saying we didn't have sex?"

"No, of course not." He sounded offended by her assumption.

"I like my women sober when they are in my bed and fully able to participate."

58

Color suffused Kenya's cheeks at Lucas's implication. "How did I get in my nightshirt?"

"Duh," he said, laughing. "I undressed you."

Kenya thought about what she'd been wearing underneath the dress and remembered—she hadn't been wearing a bra and only had on a pair of thongs. He'd gotten an eyeful.

"Don't act so prudish," Lucas said, laughing, reading her mind. "I've seen everything before."

His infectious tone made Kenya smile. He had a point. "But that didn't mean you were ever going to see it again," she responded.

"You don't say," Lucas said, reaching over with one arm to pull her back toward him until they were hip-to-hip and she felt him. "Because as I recall last night, you were very interested in an encore performance, and now that you're sober, I'm ready to oblige." He curled his fingers in her hair, lowered his head and kissed her with the passion he must have been holding inside for the last two days.

Kenya wanted to resist him, knew she should, but when his lips parted and his tongue dove inside her mouth, she forgot about her headache and all thoughts of resisting this man. Instead, she matched his heat and kissed him back, letting him know with her lips and body that she wasn't going to fight him or this any longer.

"Chynna," Lucas murmured her sister's name, but Kenya blocked it out and focused on his tender kisses.

His hands moved down her back and then lower, to stroke her thighs. He parted them, and Kenya felt the tiny scrap of a thong being pushed aside as his fingers found their way to her mound, which was already slick thanks to his hot and heavy kisses. He slid his finger in and out of her, making figure eights, and Kenya moaned aloud.

"Lucas, Lucas ..."

"Yes, love." He stopped his ministrations to look deep into her eyes.

Kenya said the words she'd told herself she wouldn't say again while she tugged at the buttons on his shirt, releasing the snaps one by one. "Make love to me." She slid the tuxedo shirt down Lucas's buff arms.

"You don't have to tell me twice." He rose on his haunches long enough to remove his T-shirt, slacks and briefs to return to her in all his naked glory. He had a foil packet between his teeth, which he used to protect them both. Then he removed her scrappy NYU T-shirt from her body. She'd thought he'd removed the thong, but he must have been as hungry for her as she was for him, because he just moved it aside, lifted her hips and plunged inside her.

Lucas cupped her bottom as he began a slow, steady rhythm of thrusting inside her all the while teasing her nipples that ached for his touch. It felt good and right. Somehow he seemed to fill the emptiness she'd never truly understood existed until now. If only she wasn't lying to him about who she really was. Kenya blocked those thoughts from her mind and focused, savoring each intensely pleasurable moment. Lucas caught her mouth in a languorous kiss. His tongue swirled inside as each thrust of his cock wound her tighter and tighter until she surrendered to the mind-blowing bliss. Minutes later, his body tensed and jerked, and then she heard Lucas's guttural cry as he climaxed inside her.

"Beautiful, sexy, exquisite Chynna," Lucas whispered, falling to his side. "I don't think I will ever get tired of making love to you."

KENYA WAS OVERCOME by his words and turned away from Lucas so he wouldn't see the tears that had suddenly sprung to her eyes. He thought she was her sister. *How could she continue to deceive him, but be true to her sister?* But how could she not tell him the truth when she'd fallen in love with him. In her heart of hearts, she knew it to be true, knew that she loved him, but they couldn't have a future with a lie hanging between them.

Suddenly, Kenya's cell phone rang, and she was thankful for the interruption. "Excuse me." Without looking at Lucas, she jumped up from her bed and pulled up a tangled sheet, swept it around her and glanced around for the clutch she'd brought with her last night. She found it on the chaise next to the dress Lucas had removed last night, and she took it into the bathroom.

She glanced down at the screen and it read *Kenya* "Chynna?" Kenya whispered into the phone. "Where have you been? I've been trying to reach you for days."

"I'm so sorry," Chynna said on the other end of the line. "But the ranch got hit with buckets of rain. Caused a flash flood over the last couple of days, and we haven't been able to leave the ranch."

"Omigod! Are you okay?" Fear suddenly coursed through Kenya.

"Yes, yes, I'm fine. We've just been holed up here at the main house. Today is the first day the sun came out, and everyone's out surveying the damage."

"I'm glad you're alright ..."

"But-"

"But we can't go on like this, Chynna." Kenya stared at the door and thought of the incredible man on the other side. The man she loved.

"I know," Chynna said, "and I'm sorry that this has dragged out longer than I said, but, Kenya, you don't understand."

"I do understand," Kenya said. "But I'd thought you'd changed or at least were starting to get it, but instead it's classic Chynna all over again. You're enjoying your life so much that you haven't given a second thought to what's going on here with me."

"That's not true. I have thought about you. Haven't you enjoyed getting time with Lucas? I thought you two were becoming close."

"Of course I have enjoyed my time," Kenya sniffed. "But he thinks I, I'm you," she said, her voice cracking under the pressure. "He-he has no idea who I really am. So our whole relationship is built on a lie."

Chynna could relate. She and Noah had started out that way, the only difference was that she'd come clean, but Kenya couldn't without revealing their entire scheme and starting a chain of events. Chynna wasn't ready to deal with that. "I'm sorry, Kenya, that I've put you in this position."

"You need to come back here and face your life," Kenya said, "so I can move on with mine. I can't live your life indefinitely."

"I never asked you to."

"Haven't you?" Kenya retorted. "Not once have you said when you're coming back, Chynna. Is that why you called me today? Were you calling to make arrangements to switch places?" The phone line remained silent. "That's what I thought. So why did you call me, Chynna? What do you want from me now?" *Why am I always the one doing the giving?*

"I, I ..." Chynna stopped, falling silent. She didn't know what to say now without appearing self-centered and completely selfish. She wanted more time with Noah, but she didn't really have the right to ask Kenya to continue the charade. She was torn.

"What is it?" Kenya pressed.

"Give me a few more days," Chynna finally spat out.

"A few more days? Are you for real?" She couldn't believe Chynna's nerve after what she'd just staid.

"Yes, give me until the end of the week, and we'll switch places before the Seattle concert."

Kenya remained silent. The end of the week seemed like an eternity. How could she keep up this farce with Lucas without giving herself away? Now that they'd gone to bed again, he wouldn't be going away quietly as he'd done in the past. He'd want her in his bed every night, and she wanted him there, but having him so close could ruin everything. "I'll think about it."

"But—"

"No 'buts', Chynna," Kenya replied. "You've had your say. I will call you and let you know my decision.'

"Fair enough. I'll wait for you call."

Seconds later, Kenya heard a dial tone and that's when she realized she hadn't told Chynna about Eli and that she suspected he was onto her. She'd never cared, that much was obvious, but last night there had been something different about him. He'd acted like he knew something she didn't. He acted like he knew the truth. Now what was she going to do about it?

KENYA's DAY didn't fare any better after her call with Chynna. When she'd exited the bathroom, she'd been hurt to see that Lucas had gone without as much as a note. It was payback considering she'd done the same thing to him. But why had he left? He must have been hurt when she hadn't echoed his same sentiment over their incredible lovemaking. She'd wanted to tell him how she felt, but she'd been so overcome with emotions that she couldn't voice them. And then Chynna had called asking for more time.

Time which apparently she no longer had. Just that morning, her agent had called and told Kenya in no uncertain terms that she needed to get her butt back to New York because the series had been called back from winter hiatus early, and she was due back in a week. Everything was coming full circle and something was going to have to give, or Kenya was going to have a nervous breakdown.

Now she was sitting on her couch listening to Deacon and Fiona break down her schedule for her upcoming show in Vegas the following day. Thanks to Chynna choosing to stay in Tucson for several more days, Kenya was going to have perform for her again, but this time it was going to be in Caesars Palace for Christ's sake! As much as Kenya had enjoyed her first foray into onstage entertainment, it was hard work and she was due back in the dance studio later that afternoon to practice a couple of new moves.

Touring was hard, and Kenya was ready to pack in her stilettos for the comfortable life she had in New York. She'd had a taste of Chynna's life, and as much as she'd enjoyed the fame, adoration, clothes and fancy cars, Kenya realized the grass was not greener on the other side. Although she may not have as much as Chynna, she enjoyed her life in New York. Unfortunately, it would not include Lucas because when she left LA, she would be leaving him behind.

Kenya longed to tell him the truth, but that wasn't possible. She would have to leave without him knowing who she was and that what they'd shared had meant something to her. Because once Chynna got back, she would give him the brush-off, which he wouldn't understand. He would be completely thrown by the sudden shift in her feelings for him, and there wasn't a thing Kenya could do. She'd brought this upon herself by agreeing to this charade to begin with. But who could have known that she would fall in love with the owner of Chynna's record label?

If anyone had told her she would have done everything she had over the last couple of weeks, she would have told them they were crazy. But she'd walked in Chynna's shoes, and she was ready to give them back except Chynna had asked her for more time. Could she continue to keep up appearances for her beleaguered twin? And did she want to?

An image of Lucas sprung in her mind. Three more days possibly meant three more nights with him. Three more nights to experience bliss in his arms. Was it worth the risk?

ELI READ the investigative report in front of him. Kenya James hadn't been seen at her apartment in weeks. Her landlord remembered her saying something about going away to a spa, but hadn't seen or heard from her since. Could the spa be the very same place Chynna had gone to escape the press after the Blake debacle?

Eli knew the answer. Yes. The two sisters had traded places. Kenya had come here to LA, which explained the drastic change in behavior since "Chynna's" return in the last few weeks. It explained why "Chynna" had suddenly become a darn good actress. Why? Because her sister, Kenya, was a seasoned actor from Broadway and an Emmy-nominated television series. Of course, Chynna hadn't suddenly gotten acting chops and become a good actress. *How could I have not seen it before?*

Kenya was playing Chynna pretty darn good, he might add, if she hadn't slipped up by being so mouthy and opinionated. *But where is Chynna? Is she still at the spa in Tucson?* He'd sent the investigator to the spa to find out. Now all he had to do was figure out how to capitalize on the twins' daring scheme and use it to his benefit.

. . .

Lucas played basketball with the young teens at the Boys and Girls Club of Carson. He'd been coming back to the center he'd frequented as a child because he felt like now that he'd succeeded, he should and could give back to the community. The youth appreciated his monthly visits, which he vowed to make more often.

But his mind wasn't on the activity today. His mind was on Chynna and her on-again, off-again behavior. He couldn't figure her out. She was an enigma. One minute he thought she was a spoiled diva. The next, she was an accomplished actress. The next, she was a sexy seductress on the dance floor. He didn't know which Chynna he was going to get at any given minute.

Last night or rather this morning, he'd thought that there would be no obstacles between them. It had been a first for him to open up and tell her how much he'd enjoyed being with her. But as soon as he'd said the words, he'd wished he could take them back because Chynna had coldly turned away from him. She'd turned away from him and had probably been looking for any easy way out without hurting his feelings. Lucky for her, her cell phone rang and interrupted the intimate the moment.

As soon as she'd gone into the bathroom, he'd high-tailed out of her bedroom right away so he could gather up his clothes strewn across the room during the heat of passion. He hadn't wanted to be there when she reemerged to avoid her giving him the kiss-off. He didn't know why that should surprise him. Chynna was the love 'em and leave 'em type, or so she'd always been portrayed. She would have been perfect for him until now. Now, he was starting to have feelings for her, but clearly he'd been fooling himself if he thought those feelings would be reciprocated or could go anywhere. Maybe that's why he'd always kept his relationships at arm's length—less chance of getting hurt that way.

. . .

"ARE you sure he's going to be at the Boys and Girls Club?" Kenya had asked Lucas's assistant.

"Yes, it's a standing appointment on his calendar. He goes there twice a month. Not to mention, he's donated thousands of dollars to the organization."

Kenya was surprised that Lucas was so giving with his time, but should she be? He'd indicated how hard it had been for him to get out of the community. Perhaps he wanted to show the youth that there was more to life than what they saw in their day-to-day world? Lucas was paying it forward, and Kenya smiled at the thought.

Her bodyguards, on the other hand, were not happy about driving to South Los Angeles and strongly advised her not to go. "I didn't ask you for your opinion," Kenya said. "You're going to drive me there because that's where I want to go."

"It's just not advisable, Ms. James. It's a tough area."

Kenya appreciated that they were just doing their jobs, and her tone softened. "That's why I have you two," she said, smiling at the football-player-size bodyguards.

"Alright, Ms. James."

After nearly an hour drive of navigating through Los Angeles traffic, they made their way to the Boys and Girls Club of Carson's Main Clubhouse. Kenya didn't see why it was so scary, at least not during the day. One of her bodyguards came around to open her door, and he glanced around each way before escorting her inside the building.

An elderly African-American woman was sitting at the desk. She had salt and pepper hair in a coiffed bun, caramel-colored skin and wore a pleasant smile. "Hello, may I help you?" she asked, glancing up at Kenya. Then she paused for several minutes to stare at Kenya. "Has anyone ever told you that you bare a close resemblance to Chynna James?"

Kenya smiled broadly. "Yes, because I *am* Chynna James."

"Oh, my Lord!" The woman clutched her chest and turned to the woman behind her. "Althea, come quick. Chynna James is here."

"What is it Martha?" The woman rose from her chair and rushed over to the counter. She stared open-mouthed at Kenya. "Well, I'll be ..." She caught herself before using an expletive.

Before Kenya realized what was happening, she was surrounded by the office staff, who wanted pictures and autographs. "I promise I will come back," Kenya said, scribbling her name on several pieces of paper and taking pictures with patrons. "But first, I need your help."

"What can we possibly do for you?" the woman named Althea asked.

"Well, I was hoping you could direct me to where Lucas Kingston is." Kenya said."Oh, Mr. Kingston," Althea answered. "He's with the seven- to fourteen-year-olds, outside on the basketball courts. We try to encourage physical fitness by increasing the numbers of hours per day that our young people participate in physical activities. Mr. Kingston is a big part of that. He's been a positive influence with these young boys."

"If you could point me in his direction," Kenya said, "I promise I'll come back and maybe sing a song." She knew just how much it would mean to this small office to say Chynna James had stopped by and given an impromptu concert.

"Oh, that would be wonderful, Ms. James. The kids just got out of school and would love it."

Kenya reached across the counter and squeezed Althea's hand. "Arrange it, and I'll be back."

Althea smiled. "Sure thing. Martha, can you show Ms. James to the basketball courts while I gather the children?" Althea moved from behind the counter and came around to Kenya's side.

"Follow me."

Kenya turned to her bodyguards, who were intent on following her. "Gentlemen."

They followed Martha outside into the blazing hot sun on the black top outside. Kenya shielded her eyes from the sun, and she saw Lucas outside showing a young boy who couldn't be more than seven or eight years old how to dribble. Martha walked toward him, but Kenya remained frozen in place.

She was nervous. She hadn't planned what she was going to say to Lucas. She only knew that she had to undo the damage she'd done earlier when he'd opened up about how much he'd enjoyed being with her. She'd been fearful of reciting the words back because she didn't have anything to offer Lucas, except more lies. Yet somehow she couldn't leave things as they were and have Lucas believe he meant nothing to her. And so, she'd gone to his office in the hopes of talking to him only to learn he'd left early for the day and come to the Boys and Girls Club.

Kenya could see Martha speaking to Lucas, and she saw him glance up to see her. Even from where she stood, his shock at seeing her was evident. He could have stayed where he was and ignored her, but instead he walked toward her.

STUNNED IS what Lucas felt when he saw Chynna standing on the basketball courts in the middle of

South Central. The Chynna he knew would never be caught dead here, so yet again, she was surprising him.

"Chynna," he said, inclining his head toward her bodyguards, who, at his presence, took several steps backward to give them some privacy. "What are you doing here?"

"I came to talk to you."

"Here?"

Kenya shrugged. "Figured I owed it to you after this morning."

Lucas turned away. "You don't owe me anything, Chynna."

Kenya reached out to touch his arm and an electric current went right through him at her touch. Why did she affect him so? "Perhaps 'owe' is the wrong word," she said. "I didn't know what to say this morning. You caught me off-guard."

Lucas turned and stared at her. "Don't you think you've done the same to me too, Chynna? You're not the same person you were before. You've changed, and for the life of me I can't figure you out. I mean, you do realize you're in South Central, right?"

Kenya chuckled. "Yes, I do. And I came for here for you."

"Why is that?" he said more sharply than he intended.

"To tell you I feel the same way," Kenya responded. "That I enjoy being with you too."

"You do?" Lucas asked.

Kenya nodded.

Lucas wasted no time encircling her in his arms and covering her mouth hungrily. He moved his mouth over hers, devouring its softness, and he would have continued kissing her if not for the tiny hand tugging on his shirt.

Lucas glanced down to see the young boy he'd been

70

teaching dribbling to. The child was staring up at him. "Are you going to help me with my dribble or are you going to play kissy-face with the pretty lady?"

Kenya laughed at the young boy's audacity as Lucas pulled away from the embrace.

"We'll have to finish this later," he told Kenya

"Sounds great."

LATER, as Kenya sang a gospel song he'd never heard to about two dozen children who'd congregated in the reading room, Lucas was amazed by how selfless and giving Chynna had become. He just never remembered her behaving this way before. That's when he was reminded by something Eli had said— that Chynna had been different since she'd come back from Tucson. Perhaps Eli was onto something, because as much as he appreciated Chynna giving an impromptu concert at the club, he just couldn't picture the Chynna of old taking time out of her day to come visit him in the hood. She'd definitely changed. And for the first time, Lucas had a nagging suspicion that perhaps Eli's instincts about Chynna's change in behaviour were right.

CHAPTER 5

The ranch was a bustle of activity, getting back to everyday normalcy after the flash flood had forced everyone indoors for two days. While Isaac and Madelyn spoke to their guests, Chynna joined Noah on horseback to check on the cattle that'd been out in the pastures and had sought higher ground during the rains. They rode up to the further part of their five hundred acres, but before they'd departed, Noah had ensured that they'd brought plenty of provisions, from water to food to most importantly, swimsuits. Noah had informed her there was an awesome lake in the mountains they could go swimming in after they'd ridden for a couple of hours to check on the cattle.

Noah checked on several cows that were pregnant and due to deliver soon and made sure the herd was accounted for before he suggested breaking for lunch. Chynna was all for it. The sun was high overhead and had been since noon. It seemed like the heat had come on with a vengeance after a couple of days reprieve. The great part was that it was still spring in the desert and would cool off in the evening.

"Ready for lunch?" Noah asked as he helped her

down and tied her palomino next to his Egyptian Arabian.

"Starved," Chynna said. Even though they'd eaten the breakfast casserole a few hours ago, she'd worked up an appetite, especially when she'd had to help him untangle a steer that'd gotten tangled in the fence. It had been heartbreaking to hear his cries, but eventually Noah had managed to wrangle him free, and he'd gone galloping out into the pasture.

"Good," Noah said, "'cause cook packed us up a great lunch." He grabbed a large duffle bag from his saddle and hers before taking her hand to lead her down a winding path.

"Where are we going?" she asked after they'd hiked several minutes down a rocky path.

Noah smiled back at her. "You'll see."

Several minutes later, they arrived at a small clearing with a great view of the mountain. In the center was a huge lake. Chynna could see tons of cacti dotting the surrounding it.

"This is beautiful, Noah. Why haven't you taken me here before?"

"Hasn't been time," he said. "Plus I figured since we were coming this far out, we might as well enjoy it."

"Do you come here often?"

"We used to when we were kids," Noah answered, pulling out a blanket from his duffle and laying it out the ground. "We would come out here as a family to go camping, canoeing or kayaking. We had the best time."

Chynna smiled as she sat beside him on the blanket. "Sounds like fun." She'd never been much into the outdoors as she didn't like bugs, but she could appreciate the beauty.

"It was," Noah said, "Maya and I—..." He cut his sentence short as soon as he said her name.

Chynna reached across the short distance between

them to touch his arm. "You don't have to stop talking about her, Noah," she said quietly. "She was a big part of your life, and you can't act like she didn't exist, and I wouldn't expect you to."

A tentative smile spread on Noah's lips, and he patted her hand back. "Thank you. I appreciate that."

"So you and Maya used to do what?" Chynna asked.

"We would come up here fishing," Noah answered, "but she was terrible at it." He laughed as if remembering a memory. "So eventually we started coming less and less and when she passed ..." He paused, then picked up, "I stopped coming altogether."

"Why's that?"

Noah shrugged and looked over the mountainous landscape. "Guess the memories hurt too much."

"And now?"

He glanced at her with an intent expression. "Now, I have a reason to."

Chynna was speechless. She felt like he wanted to say more, but held back.

"Ready for that sandwich?"

"Yes, sir."

Noah pulled out two hearty, thick-sliced ham and cheese sandwiches covered in Saran wrap and offered her one. Chynna greedily accepted and they ate in silence, both too afraid to say how they truly felt.

Chynna's time was winding down at Golden Oaks, and she wasn't sure what she could offer Noah after she left and whether he wanted to continue seeing her at all, so she chose to say nothing.

Afterward, Noah suggested they change into their swimsuits for a quick dip in the lake. Chynna didn't have anything with her except the bikinis she'd brought with her for her stay at Canyon Ranch. Despite the fact that Noah had seen her naked and knew every part of her, Chynna changed behind a bush. When she emerged, Noah was bare-chested and wearing a pair of blue swim shorts. Chynna swallowed, and her loins tightened when she looked at the hair lightly dotting his chest.

Noah wasn't faring much better. He seemed like he was ready to swallow her whole if the hungry look he was giving her in her leopard-print bikini was any indication. "C'mon," he said, running toward the lake and jumping right in.

"Noah," Chynna said, laughing when the water splashed her as she came toward the lake's edge.

"Come in," he said, wiping water from his eyes as he treaded water. "It feels great."

Chynna made a more graceful entrance and eased her way into the lake and swam toward him.

Noah was waiting for her and wrapped his arms around her waist. "That's more like it," he said and lowered his head to kiss her. The caress of his lips on hers set her body aflame with longing. He spun her around in the water as she kissed him back with equal passion. His hands roamed down her side and hips to finally rest on her butt. He pressed her firmly to him and through his shorts, Chynna could feel his erection. She rubbed herself against his hot center, and Noah groaned.

"Chynna," he whispered, undoing the tie on her halter bikini top to release her breasts from their confines. His bent his head so he could tongue and caress her already swollen nipples.

Chynna's head went back of its own volition. She grasped his head to her breasts as he licked and teased the buds into hardened peaks. She wrapped her legs around his waist, and Noah took the hint, and soon he was lifting her out of the water and bringing her back to the blanket.

He gently eased her wet body down just as he

76

showed the other breast equal attention. Chynna curled into his body, and Noah moved from her breasts down her silken belly to hook his fingers into her bikini bottoms and slide the wet material down her legs. He tossed them and his swim trunks aside in quick succession to rejoin her on the blanket. He rose on his haunches, spreading her legs, but then he paused above her.

"Christ, I forgot a condom," Noah said.

"It's okay," Chynna moaned. "I'm on the pill."

Noah paused as if milling the thought over.

"I've been tested if that's what you're concerned about." Chynna glanced up into Noah's eyes. They glowed with passion, "And I—I haven't been with anyone in quite some time." She knew the press reported she was the sort of woman that wasn't particular about whom she took to bed, but she was and she always practiced safe sex. Even that drunken night with her dancer, she'd insisted on protection.

Noah brushed her hair back so he could stare deep into her eyes. "I don't think I could resist you if I tried." He kissed her with a hunger that showed her he cared more about her than he was willing to admit, just as he pressed forward and thrust inside her.

Chynna accepted him willingly, lovingly. She kissed his neck and his earlobe as he thrust further for a deeper connection. She cried out at the intense feeling of having him buried inside her. At that moment, it was just the two of them, out in the open, being one with not just nature, but with each other. She locked her ankles around his waist and circled her arms around his neck to match his thrust. Each rhythm and motion brought them closer to the peak, to the edge of ecstasy, but just as she neared it, Noah would slow the rhythm down.

It was exquisite torture, and Chynna wished the

moment could last forever, before reality would tear them apart. Her urgent sighs pleaded with Noah, and he answered them. Her release hit her like a killer wave, and she tried swimming to the surface, but the current carried her away. When he reached his peak, Noah shuddered once, twice, three times. He trembled above her before he collapsed onto his side as he too lost his grip with reality.

EVENTUALLY, he and Chynna rose, rinsed off in the lake before dressing, and they began returning to the ranch. As he rode back, Noah couldn't remember a time in which he'd been so free with his sexuality. He hated to compare the women, but he didn't have a whole lot of experience to compare it to, seeing as how he'd only been with two women in his life: Maya and Chynna. And Maya, well he'd always wanted to make love outside, but Maya had been shy and hadn't wanted to, in case they got caught.

But Chynna, she was so liberated and free that she'd embraced making love with him in the open. She was a breath of fresh air that Noah was fast becoming used to, which could be a problem. As much as he didn't want to think about, he knew she couldn't stay on at the ranch indefinitely, but as long as she was here, he intended on enjoying her. It was just that this fun, sexy, beautiful woman had touched his heart and gotten to him like no woman ever had. The thought of her leaving scared the living daylights out of him, but the thought of her staying and what would come next was equally as scary.

· · ·

78

LATER, after the family had eaten dinner and was sitting at the dining room table, Caleb announced, "I'm tired of this place."

"Already, Caleb?" Madelyn asked. "You just got here."

"And I was promptly sequestered for two days," he responded. "It's time for some fun. Who's game?" He looked at Noah, then Rylee and Chynna. "Come on. Don't tell me you enjoy long nights by the fire with the parental units."

Rylee couldn't resist a chuckle. "Well, now that you mention it, I could use a night out on the town."

"Why don't you take Jeremy?" their father suggested.

"No, thank you, Daddy," Rylee huffed. "I actually want to *have fun.*"

"Then let's go boot scooting," Caleb said, rising from the table and nearly knocking down his chair. "We'll go into town to the saloon."

"I'm game," Rylee said, standing and turning to Chynna and Noah, still sitting at the table. "Don't be spoilsports. Come on, you two."

"Are you sure I should??" Chynna asked. "What if someone recognizes me?"

"In this town?" Caleb asked. "I sincerely doubt it. Most folks here listen to country. The only reason I recognized you is because Rylee plays your music all the dang time."

Rylee huffed and folded her arms across her chest. "I do not!"

Chynna was hesitant. "I don't know…"

"It'll be fine," Rylee said, "C'mon we have to get out of this place."

"I agree." Noah jumped to his feet and turned to Chynna. "How about it? You ready to line dance?"

Chynna knew when she was outnumbered and let

go of her misgivings. She rose to her feet and said. "Have you seen my videos? I'm an excellent dancer."

"Oh, baby," Noah said. "Line dancing is nothing like booty shaking." Everyone laughed as they, Caleb and Rylee left the room.

A half hour later, Rylee and Chynna had changed clothes and shoes, the men preferring to keep the jeans and button-down shirts they'd been wearing on. Rylee wore boyfriend jeans, an embellished T-shirt and a princess blue cropped jacket with red leather boots that reached her knees, while Chynna had shimmed her way into skinny silver jeans and a cutout sweater top with a slashed black.

Noah gave Chynna a once-over in the skintight shiny jeans she wore, but didn't comment as she and Rylee slid into Noah's pickup truck and headed into town for a night of fun. It was a short drive to the nearby saloon on the outskirts of town, but was quite crowded. Chynna was surprised given that it was a Thursday night.

"Ladies night," Rylee indicated as they walked into the room and saw tons of women walking around in jeans with cowboy boots and hats.

"Just how I like it!" Caleb said. "Excuse me while I go have some fun." Seconds later, he was gone.

"Wow!" Rylee said as she looked at his retreating figure. "I thought I would have a dance partner."

"Did you really?" Noah gave her a knowing look.

Rylee laughed. "Okay, wishful thinking,"

"How about some drinks, ladies?" Noah asked.

"Love one," they both said in unison. Chynna glanced wistfully at Noah as he walked away—a look that Rylee caught.

"Is everything okay?"

"Yeah, why do you ask?" Chynna said, staring at Noah. She noticed several women leaning against the bar, giving him their best come-hither looks. The great part was she didn't have to wonder about Noah's loyalty. He was a man who would never cheat on her like so many of the other men she'd dated in Hollywood.

"I dunno. You looked a little sad when Noah walked away."

"Maybe just a little," Chynna admitted.

"Why? Has he done something wrong?"

Chynna shook her head. "No, things actually couldn't be better between us."

"Then what gives?" Rylee asked, peering up at her.

"I'm just worried about what happens next."

"You mean when you have to leave?"

Chynna nodded. "Noah and I haven't discussed what happens later or whether he would even be open to a long-distance relationship."

"My brother is not the casual relationship type."

"True," Chynna conceded, "but I doubt he's ready to be Mr. Chynna James and follow me on the road either. His life is here."

"You have a point, which is why you need to talk to him rather than brood. Get it out in the open, clear the air."

"I know you're right," Chynna said, "but I'm scared about what happens *after* we've had the talk. It'll change everything."

"Isn't it worse not knowing?"

Chynna laughed. "Sometimes ignorance is bliss."

Noah returned to the table they'd procured with three beer bottles in his hand. Chynna wasn't much of a beer drinker, but the saloon struck her as the type that wouldn't make martinis.

"Thank you," she said, accepting the beer bottle and taking a nervous swig.

"So what were you two talking about when I came over?" Noah asked, glancing back and forth between the two women. "From across the room it looked intense."

"You, you dope." Rylee punched him in the arm.

"Well, then that's an acceptable topic," he said, laughing and taking a large swig of his beer, though Noah suspected there was more to the story than Rylee was telling him. After they'd made love near the lake, Chynna had been unusually quiet. He suspected she was thinking about what would come next, just as he was, but they both were too scared to broach the subject.

"I, for one, didn't come here to stand on the sidelines," Rylee said, putting down her bottle of beer and taking a step toward the dance floor, where a crowd had already formed to start the next line dance. "I'm going to dance. Y'all coming?" she asked, turning to glance at them.

"You go ahead," Noah said. "We'll be right behind you."

"Alright," Rylee said and sashayed her way onto the dance floor. It didn't take long for his not-so-shy sister to disappear into the crowd.

"So, do you want to talk about what's on your mind?" Noah asked, chartering into dangerous territory.

Chynna glanced at him and took another swig of beer. "Do you?"

Noah shrugged. "Not really, but I know we need to talk."

"And we'll talk later." Chynna chugged more of her beer before placing it on the table. "For now, let's dance!" She grabbed Noah by the hand, barely giving him time to set his beer down before leading him to the dance floor.

Chynna had a great time dancing with Noah and attempting to learning all the line dances that went with each song. She was great at choreography and pretty soon was picking up most of the moves while Noah struggled with two left feet.

"How do you pick it up so fast?" Noah asked, out of breath when they finally paused to take a break. Rylee was still on the dance floor, and Caleb was sidled up next to a six-foot tall, big-breasted brunette wearing a miniskirt with a tube top and red cowboy boots.

Chynna shrugged. "It's a gift, I suppose. I've always been good with dancing. When we were younger in tap and jazz, I would catch on quickly while Kenya, on the other hand, always had to practice, practice, practice."

"Well, I'm much better at slow dancing anyway," Noah whispered seductively in her ear as he pulled her closer to his frame.

"Is that a fact?" Chynna teased, glancing up at him through flirty lashes.

"Oh, just wait to you see my moves."

Noah showed her not only his slow dance moves at the saloon, but he showed her just how gentle and loving he could be when they got back to the ranch, and he made achingly slow love with her until her toes curled with satisfaction. Chynna didn't want the night to end because in the pit of her stomach, she felt the world shifting on its axis, and her world was about to change and this time it would be out of her control.

CHAPTER 6

*K*enya was having a hard time picking up the new dance routine as usual. Given they were in Vegas, the choreographer had added a new element to the opening sequence, and she was having a hard time remembering it. She supposed her lack of focus could be from the fact that she and Lucas had stayed up nearly all night making love.

"Give me a minute, okay?" Kenya said, leaving the stage at the Caesars Palace where they were practicing for Chynna's show later that evening. Kenya smiled as she passed her bodyguards and hotel security and headed toward her dressing room. Once there, she closed the door with a sigh. Her mind wasn't on dancing, it was on Lucas.

Showing up at the Boys and Girls Club had been a breakthrough for her and Lucas. Lucas had been shocked that she'd come there looking for him and not to walk away but to embrace their relationship. He didn't know that the reason Kenya had been so bold was because she knew this would be the last day they would be spending together.

She wasn't Chynna, and she could no longer keep living her sister's life. She had to reclaim her own life.

Coming here, she'd learned that the old adage that all that glitters isn't gold was true. With all the glitz and glamour, Chynna's life was no better than her life in New York. Sure, she had the cars, clothes and jewels, but Kenya had come to realize just unhappy her sister had been with all of it. She'd run away from her own life because it was suffocating and she'd lost her identity.

For a moment, she'd allowed herself to get caught up in Chynna's world, in her drama and as a result, she'd fallen for Lucas. He was the one real thing she'd found in Chynna's world, but even that was built on a lie. He thought she was her sister for Christ's sake. He thought he'd fallen for the spoiled diva that'd had a sudden transformation.

And why? Because she'd deceived him. Once Lucas learned the truth, he would never forgive the lies, the betrayal, and the deception. New York wouldn't be far enough away to escape the wrath she knew was sure to follow. She had to get out now.

She walked over to Chynna's Louis Vuitton purse, reached inside and pulled out her cell phone.

"Kenya," Chynna answered on the first ring. "I've been waiting for your call."

"Good, because I have an answer for you."

"You're ready to switch places," Chynna said.

"Yes." Kenya nodded and stared at her reflection in the mirror. With the honey-blond highlights, cropped top and tight leggings, she could hardly recognize herself anymore.

There was silence on the other end of the line, and Kenya wondered if her twin had hung up on her until Chynna asked, "When?"

"Tomorrow," Kenya said. "I'll tell everyone that I'm staying in Vegas for another day. That'll give you enough time to make flight arrangements and get here so we can switch places."

"Alright," Chynna said. "I will call you once I've booked a flight, and we'll talk strategy."

"Good," Kenya said, letting out an audible sigh. "I'm sorry I couldn't give you more time, but even you must see that this is for the best. We are getting in too deep, and this will blow up in our faces."

"I understand," Chynna replied softly. "I've asked a lot of you, twinie, and I won't ask for anymore. We'll talk soon."

Seconds later, Kenya heard a dial tone. She ended the call and stared into the mirror. Time for one more performance and then she would finally hang her stilettos on the shelf.

ELI STARED at the investigator standing in front of him. He'd told the man as soon as he got cold hard facts to track him down, no matter the place or time of day. Eli had no idea just how juicy the information would be that the investigator had retrieved.

"So you mean to tell me that Chynna has been staying at this Golden Oaks Ranch for the last month, incognito?" Eli asked.

The investigator nodded. "I had to do a lot of convincing to get one of the maids who'd cleaned her villa at Canyon Ranch to give up the goods, because the manager sure wasn't going to talk. Apparently your girl checked out a few weeks ago. She came back with some rancher girl dressed in jeans and a cowboy hat to retrieve her things. Luckily, the maid who'd been cleaning the villa overheard them talking about the ranch."

"And the manager wasn't surprised by Chynna checking out?"

The investigator shook his head. "Apparently Golden Oaks has a stellar reputation as one of the best dude ranches in Arizona, if you like that sort of thing."

"And Chynna does?" Eli was amazed. Chynna had always struck him as a city girl and couldn't picture her enjoying the outdoor life and choosing to stay on a dude ranch. It didn't make sense. "Why would she stay?"

"Well," the investigator said, "local gossip in the town has her cozying up to Noah Hart, the son of the ranch's owner. He's been a grieving widower for some time."

"And in comes Chynna to heal the pain." Eli rubbed his chin. "I couldn't have asked for a better story if I'd written it myself."

"She's been staying on the ranch with the Hart family, and folks even saw them kissing on the dance floor at the ranch's thirty-fifth anniversary party this past week and dancing at the local saloon."

Eli turned to stare at him. "Any pictures?" His mind was already whirling with how he could best use Chynna's charade to his advantage. And if he couldn't, he would ensure it blew up in her face. In this day in and age, bad publicity was good publicity and would put Chynna back in the spotlight where he liked her. And it would teach her a lesson about playing games with him. *Who does she think she is anyway to think she can get away with pulling off such an elaborate scheme?*

But she had. She'd outfoxed him. And Lucas. Poor schmuck. Eli chuckled to himself. His boy thought he'd fallen for Chynna James, and instead he'd gotten bamboozled by the runner-up, her twin, Kenya. He felt bad for him, but not enough to tell him what was coming. He'd tried to tell Lucas that something hadn't been right with "Chynna" since her return from Arizona, and he'd blown him off. Now Lucas would have to find out like the rest of America—on the front page of the tabloids.

KENYA GAVE her performance that night her all. It was her swan song, so to speak, the last night she'd be on-stage imitating her sister, and Kenya had savored it like a fine wine. She'd sung her sister's most popular songs with the screams of her adoring fans in her ears. She'd danced her heart out with Chynna's fabulous dancers as if her life depended on it. She'd ensured the band and her backup singers got multiple rounds of applause for their efforts that night. And when it was all over and she'd sung Chynna's signature song, Kenya had taken a long bow.

Kenya was sure everyone thought she was being dramatic for effect, but the emotions in the moment were real. This marked the end of a journey for her and she hoped it was a new beginning. She'd found herself in LA and stopped being jealous of her younger sister. Kenya had gained a newfound confidence that she hadn't had before. And for the first time since she could remember, she'd felt beautiful and sexy. Lucas had done that for her. He'd made her feel more alive than any man had, and she would always be grateful for that, though she doubted Lucas would feel the same.

Afterward, as she walked offstage, picking up the train of her gunmetal gray custom-Armani gown, slinky with an off-center cut along the bustline, Lucas was waiting for her as were Deacon, Fiona and Penelope. On cue, Penelope handed her an Evian.

Despite all their hovering, Kenya would miss these people that had flitted like flies every day in her orbit. She broke open the cap of the water bottle and drank generously.

"Great show!" Deacon gave her a high-five.

"You were magnificent, as always," Fiona beamed.

"Thank you," Kenya said, nodding.

Lucas approached and kissed her cheek. "Hey, beautiful."

Kenya smiled at him, but didn't miss the look of disapproval from Deacon. She knew she was treading on dangerous ground, but she was powerless to resist the pull whenever she was around Lucas. "Hey yourself," she said as she continued to walk toward her dressing room.

"You were amazing," Lucas said. "We should go out to celebrate."

Kenya stopped when she made it to her dressing room. "Not tonight, babe. I'm exhausted." She feigned tiredness.

"We're in Vegas!" Lucas said. "You can't go to bed," he added, glancing at his Rolex watch, "before midnight."

"Who says?"

"I say," Lucas said. "And I'm not taking no for an answer, so go change your clothes, and I'll be waiting out here for you." He patted her on the behind as she entered her dressing room.

"Fine," she said and closed the door behind her.

LUCAS STARED AT THE DOOR. Something was off. He'd sensed it from the moment they'd arrived in Vegas. Even though they'd shared an amazing night in bed, he could feel Chynna pulling away from him, pulling away from everyone. She'd been quiet, pensive even. During the show, she'd given a stellar performance, but in his opinion, it had almost been like it was her last. He couldn't put his finger on it, but that last bow on stage had felt eerie. Perhaps he was imagining things. He had to be. Chynna had a long tour ahead of her and he hoped a long stretch of sharing his bed.

He was hooked and couldn't get enough of her. So much so that he'd tossed aside the comments Eli had made about Chynna acting different since her return from Arizona, though he had to admit her coming to the Boys and Girls Club had rattled him. He hadn't seen that one coming. Perhaps something profound had happened to her while in Arizona, causing her to reevaluate her life and how she was living it. It was certainly plausible. Lucas couldn't wrap his mind around another reason for Chynna's sudden change in behavior, but the truth of the matter was he liked the new Chynna. She was not only talented—he'd always known that—but she was more real, down to earth, and approachable than she'd ever been. He wouldn't want her to go back to the closed-off superficial woman he'd known before she left. This new Chynna was a woman he could love— a woman he might very well have fallen for now.

ELI LICKED his lips and rubbed his hands in anticipation of the fallout that was about to come. Chynna had underestimated him. She thought she could get away with tricking him by sending her sister back in her place. Well, she was in for a rude awakening. He was going to teach her a lesson that *he* ruled her. She couldn't just go off on her own and hook up with some rancher unless it was beneficial to her brand and thereby his pocketbook.

He'd ensured her rise to fame by carefully crafting her image as the next Beyoncé or Rihanna, and he wasn't about to let her tank it because she'd had a change of heart. He needed her out on the road, on stage doing what she did best—belting out songs he'd selected from the album and gyrating a body he'd made sure she kept fit.

Now, he had to remind her who was boss by sending the wolf pack after her, because that's exactly what the paparazzi would be when they smelled scandal. Sure, the publicity from the reveal that there had been an imposter in Chynna's place might seem bad to some, because Kenya had been able to successfully imitate Chynna without anyone being the wiser. But Eli was gambling that it might also make people curious about the diva and go out and buy her music. He was certain he would see a spike in ticket sales, because they'd want to see the "real" Chynna on stage.

And so he'd called one of the slimy reporters he kept on his cell phone and anonymously revealed that the real Chynna was in Tucson and the "fake" Chynna had been in her place. The reporter hadn't understood until Eli had reminded him that Chynna had an identical twin. The comment set the reporter off, and he'd started firing questions at Eli, which he evaded. He didn't say how long her twin had been impersonating Chynna— he would just let the paparazzi take it from there. Once they smelled blood, they'd be relentless for the truth.

Eli did feel bad for Lucas though. He hated to ambush him and not give him a heads-up, but the paps would need genuine emotion and having them ask him if he was with the real Chynna was just too priceless. The reporter had agreed that if everything checked out, he'd wire the money to the usual personal account Eli had set up. Eli would pocket the fifty thousand dollars they were paying him—as he'd done on previous occasions in which he'd ratted out Chynna—into his rainy day fund for the day when he might have to leave town in a hurry.

· · ·

As MUCH AS Kenya didn't want to go out with the group — Lucas, Deacon, Penelope, Fiona, her choreographer and a few of her dancers—she eventually acquiesced. And halfway through the evening, she was having a blast. They'd pigged out on one of the many late-night buffets Vegas had to offer before casino hopping at the Venetian, Caesars Place and the Paris hotel.

Kenya wasn't much for gambling, because losing her hard- earned money, which had been hard to come by, was a tough pill to swallow; but spending a little bit of Chynna's money for fun wouldn't hurt anyone. The best part was she was starting to win at Blackjack.

"I didn't know you were that good at Blackjack," Lucas whispered in her ear.

"Neither did I," Kenya said, laughing and pointing to the dealer to hit her. When she received two cards of the same value, she split and asked him to hit her again. She won both hands and scored another thousand dollars.

"Woohoo!" Fiona yelled behind her. "You are hot tonight, girlfriend."

"Yeah, you are," Deacon said disdainfully.

Kenya heard the slight note of shock in Deacon's tone and glanced back at him. Kenya pushed back from the table. She'd better not have too much fun and raise further suspicion, especially when she was so close to the finish line. By tomorrow, she would be back in New York to her own life, and her time as Chynna would all be a memory.

At nearly four am, Kenya and Lucas returned to her suite at the Bellagio in which they'd rented out the entire floor for Chynna and her entourage. Kenya was exhausted, and Lucas took over putting the hotel swipe card to the door and letting them inside. The room was dark, save for the streaming lights of the Vegas strip shining through the floor to ceiling windows that faced the famous fountain.

Kenya walked over to the window and looked out over the strip. Through the window, she saw Lucas's reflection as he removed his jacket and unbuttoned the cuffs on his shirt as he walked toward her. She tried not to tense when he placed his hands over her shoulders and brushed her hair aside to place a tender kiss on her neck. He teased the sensitive part of her nape with his tongue as his hands encircled her waist and pulled her closer to him. She felt the bulge in his pants as he ground himself against her backside.

She leaned back into his embrace and as one hand fondled her breasts, the other began loosening the straps on the bustier she'd been wearing until it fell to the floor. Then she felt a rush of air hit her thigh as that same free hand began to hike the leather miniskirt further up so one of his hands could reach inside the cheeky panties she was wearing and begin teasing her with his fingers.

It was erotic to see their reflection in the window as Lucas began stroking her slow at first and then faster and faster until her breath began to hitch and red-hot flames of desire began to course through her veins. He leaned around to kiss her closed eyelids and nose before making his way to her mouth. It was open with anticipation of his hot wet tongue, and Lucas easily satisfied her needs by making love to her mouth while his hands brought her to a climax.

"Lucas," she moaned as the sensations began to shake her entire body.

"Yes, babe ... come for me," he urged, sliding his finger faster and faster inside her until her legs began to tremble. That's when Lucas lifted her off her feet and placed her on the nearby desk. She wanted him just as bad; she needed to be with him one last time before their worlds would forever be altered. She reached for the buckle on the belt of his pants to help free that piece of him that she wanted so desperately inside her, to fill her completely.

Lucas fumbled, sliding his pants down and getting a condom on while Kenya circled her arms around his nape and pressed hot kisses on his neck and earlobe.

"Dear God, Chynna!" he groaned, lifting her hips slightly off the desk so he could thrust inside her.

"Sweet Jesus!" she moaned when Lucas entered her. It was heaven and hell all at once, because she knew she would never again find this with another man. Why? Because if she admitted the truth to herself, she loved Lucas, but she had to give him up because there would be no future for them once she left. He believed he was in love with Chynna, not her. Kenya blocked the thoughts out of her head as Lucas began to move inside her. She met his thrust by undulating her hips until they formed a steady, dizzying rhythm. It was lusty and hot, and Kenya wished it could go on forever. Her fingernails dug into his back, urging him onward.

LUCAS PLUNGED ALL the way deep inside Kenya. She felt so good, so right. She was so open, so willing to give herself to him that Lucas lost himself in the physical connection he had with this woman. He couldn't deny that she'd gotten under his skin in a big way, and he was determined to make her remember him and his body buried inside her and never think of another man.

"Oh, it feels so good," Kenya said.

He covered her mouth with his, kissing her deeply as his lower half drove deeper to seat himself inside her. He could feel her body straining for a release, but he withdrew and slowed the rhythm down, wanting to make the moment last.

When Kenya wrapped her legs around his waist to urge him onward, beads of sweat began to form on his forehead, and he lifted her off the desk and walked them to the couch so he could lay her body over it and thrust inside her once more.

This time, he hit the spot and her orgasmic cry filled the room as she tensed underneath him. The aftershocks of her lush contractions triggered his own release that he'd been restraining. Heat suffused his body, and he gave a loud shout as he collapsed on top of her.

The position was uncomfortable, and he shifted until they tumbled in a heap on the floor with Chynna on top of him. He wrapped Chynna tight in his arms, feeling possessive as he continued to shudder from the force of his orgasm. Tomorrow he would have to figure out what came next between them because one thing he was clear—Chynna James was his.

CHAPTER 7

*I*n the wee hours of the morning, Chynna slid out of Noah's bed to her room to pack. She knew it was a coward's way out, but she was afraid of the alternative, facing Noah with the fact that it was time for her to go. They'd both been afraid to broach the issue even though he too had to know that she couldn't stay at Golden Oaks Ranch. Instead, they'd buried their heads in the sand and acted like it didn't exist. And now, the jig was up.

Kenya had told her in no uncertain terms that she was ready to go back to her life, which meant that Chynna would have to go back and face all those old demons that she'd left behind. She would have to go back and stand up for herself and what she believed in. She would have to go back and write and sing music she felt strongly about and not what Eli or anyone else thought was right for her. It was time for her take her life back.

Her time here had shown her that she was much stronger than she thought and that she could do anything she set her mind to even if that meant going to battle with her record label. Look at what she'd done here: She'd rounded up cattle and helped Rylee deliver a horse in the middle of a flood, for Christ's sake!

She'd called for a car, and the driver would be coming within the hour to pick her up. Chynna hated to leave this way, but she didn't know of any other choice. If she waited until everyone else was up and said her goodbyes to the Hart family, it would be much worse.

She would say goodbye to Lila, the horse she'd seen delivered, and that would give her just enough time to go inside to talk Noah before the car arrived. Once she closed the two suitcases from the spa that Kenya had left, since Kenya had taken back Chynna's luggage, Chynna glanced at the bedroom that had been her home for the last month. She would miss the place. Golden Oaks Ranch had been the one place that had felt like home since Chynna had been discovered and left Tennessee for LA.

She closed the door, quietly crept down the steps and outside the Hart home. She took the luggage to the bottom of the steps and went to the stables so she could have a look at Lila one final time before she left.

As if sensing her presence, when she opened the stable door, Lila perked up and out of the stall. Chynna smiled and came over to rub Lila's head. The horse nuzzled against her.

"I will miss you," Chynna said.

"And will you miss me?"

Startled, Chynna jumped back long enough to see Noah standing in the doorway of the stables with a look of disbelief on his face.

"Noah!"

Hurt was etched across his features. "Were you even going to tell me goodbye?"

Chynna dropped her hands to her side and began

walking toward him, but he stepped backward. Tears sprung to her eyes. "I planned to."

"When? When you were in the car and waving goodbye?" He asked bitterly.

"I was about to come and find you."

"So th-that's it?" His voice broke. "It's over?"

"Honestly, I don't know, Noah," Chynna said, wiping an errant tear that slid down her cheek with the back of her hand. "And I've been scared to find out. Guess it was easier to live in denial of the inevitable."

"Which is?"

"That I have to go back to LA and resume my life. Even you must have known I couldn't stay here forever. My sister has been imitating me for damn near a month, and she's fed up. Told me to get my butt back home. And I have to go. She's done enough for me already."

Noah swallowed. "I understand that, Chynna, but we could have talked about this."

"And?" she let the word dangle in the air.

"And figure something out."

"Like what?" she asked, folding her arms across her chest.

"Are you ready for a long distance relationship? Are you ready for the scrutiny that comes with dating 'Chynna James,' the star," she said, making quotation mark signs with her hands, "I promise you the press is relentless. They will hound you endlessly if they think we're together."

"And you don't think I can handle them?" Noah asked.

"I didn't know you would want to," Chynna said. "And I was afraid to find out. But I guess there's no better time than the present to ask. What do you want, Noah? Where do you see this relationship going?"

Just then, they heard a lot of commotion and loud

voices outside the stable door. Noah was closest and rushed to the door with Chynna on his heels. They stumbled right into the flashbulbs of a dozen members of the press standing outside the Hart stables with cameras and microphones.

One of them pressed a microphone toward Chynna's face.

"Chynna, is it true you've been holed up here with Noah Hart while your twin's been imitating you for weeks?"

Stunned, Chynna turned to Noah, who she could see was overwhelmed by the sheer amount of people gathered around them and cameras flashing pictures of him and his family's home. In that moment, she knew it was over, knew that he wasn't ready for a life in the limelight, and she couldn't ask him to live under its scrutiny. He belonged here at the ranch with his family, and he deserved a woman that would fit into that role.

Chynna spied the car she'd hired sitting in front of the main house. She would have to make a break for it. Of course, that was easier said than done, especially now that she didn't have her two huge bodyguards with her for an easy getaway.

"Excuse me," she said, pushing past the throng of reporters screaming at her and taking pictures. Noah followed behind her and was able to keep some of them at bay as she made her way to the vehicle.

Noah made it to the Lincoln Town Car first and opened the car door for her. Chynna quickly rushed inside and slammed the door. Then she rolled down the window long enough to mouth, "I'm sorry."

Then she rolled it back up and yelled at the driver to take off. Her luggage be damned, she was under fire and this was just the beginning.

. . .

NOAH STARED at the vehicle as the dust sputtered in the air from it, speeding away. The reporters swarmed around him, each trying to get a picture of him, Chynna James's newest conquest. But Noah didn't care. In the blink of any eye, Chynna was gone. Just as she'd sped into his life in a blaze of glory, she'd sped right out of it.

He turned to the reporters and yelled, "This is private property. Get off my land before I have you all arrested." He started for the main house. When one of the reporters followed, Noah turned quickly as if daring him to take another step. Instead, the reporter snapped another quick photograph before rushing away so he could no doubt chase Chynna's car down the freeway.

As he approached the house, Noah saw his mother, father, Caleb and Rylee standing in their robes on the porch. They wore looks of shock, disbelief and pity. It was the look of pity he hated the most.

As he walked by, Caleb touched his arm, but Noah shook him off and pointed his index finger at him. "Not a word." Once inside, he slammed the door behind him.

KENYA HAD her escape all planned. During the mêlée of everyone preparing to depart for the airport, Kenya would sneak away. She'd paid the room steward a hundred bucks so she could leave through the service entrance so no one would be the wiser.

Sure enough her plan worked perfectly. After giving her a long, deep kiss, Lucas had departed from her bed earlier that morning to pack and make a few phone calls. She went about her day as normal, showering and changing into a Chynna outfit of skinny jeans with a lace peplum shirt and heels and waited for her moment.

It came when the hotel bellman knocked on her suite door for their luggage. The bodyguards were preoccupied with them. While Deacon and Penelope were so busy talking details about the day, they didn't see Kenya slip out the side door. It was time to make her move. The meager items she'd taken with her since Arizona had been packed into a duffle bag. Kenya pulled out a baseball cap from her purse and donned some large sunglasses. It was perfect—no one would recognize her.

Proud of her handiwork, Kenya made her way for the elevator.She had no idea that the investigator Eli had hired was watching her every move and had just notified the press of her impending departure.

ONCE OUT THE ELEVATOR, Kenya made her way toward the service entrance. The room steward was waiting for her and led her through the service area and, she hoped, toward the door to freedom. What greeted her, however, when she opened the door to the outside, was a throng of reporters with microphones in their hands.

"Kenya, how long have you been imitating your sister, Chynna?"

"Who came up with the idea to switch places?"

"Why did you agree to the switch?"

Terrified, Kenya closed the door and locked it behind her. *Dear God, we've been exposed! How in the world could this have happened after we'd been so careful?* She'd been so close to getting back to her own life without anyone being the wiser. Kenya backed away from the door and the loud voices from outside.

What was she going to do? And how was she going to get out of there?

. . .

"CALM DOWN, KENYA," Chynna said on the other end of the line.

"How can I be calm?" Kenya whispered angrily. "I have reporters waiting outside the hotel ready to rip me to pieces."

"Where are you?"

"I'm in the ladies room," Kenya said. After the fiasco outside, she'd run to the only place they wouldn't follow her.

"I know this is crazy," Chynna said, "but I need you to stay calm. I'm in the same boat. They ambushed me as well. And ...," she said, glancing behind her, "are following me on the freeway as we head to the airport. Give me a minute to make some calls, and I will get you out of there."

"Chynna, this is a mess," Kenya cried.

Chynna sighed, "I know, and it's all my fault. Just give me a few minutes to figure things out and make arrangements, okay? But I promise you I won't leave you in the lurch. You can count on me."

"Promise?"

"I promise," Chynna said, ending the call. She leaned back against the cushions in the backseat. She was in such hot water, she didn't know how she was going to get out of this one. She'd never counted on anyone finding out the truth and therefore hadn't made backup arrangements. She hadn't told anyone of her plan, and now everyone was going to feel scorned. *Is anyone going to help me?*

LUCAS STARED at the television in his hotel room in stunned silence. He couldn't believe what he was seeing. He'd been on a phone call with a distributor when they'd advised him to turn on the television. That's when he'd seen the late-breaking news that Chynna

James and her twin, Kenya James, had traded places. It was reported that the sisters had done so after a spa getaway at Canyon Ranch, and that's where they'd hatched the plan. Kenya returned to Los Angeles in Chynna's place while Chynna stayed in Tucson and, as luck would have it, hooked up with widowed rancher Noah Hart. A photograph was displayed with a guy wearing a cowboy hat.

Lucas stepped backward and fell down into a nearby armchair, loosening his tie. *Chynna isn't Chynna?* So, he hadn't been falling for Chynna, he'd been falling for her sister, Kenya? *Who in the hell would concoct such a lie?* Immediately he thought of Eli. He'd always thought that Chynna hadn't been right since she'd come back from Arizona. *But has he been right all along?*

Lucas recalled how unusual it had been for Chynna to show up to the Boys and Girls Club and how happy yet uneasy he'd felt by her surprise appearance. He recalled how great Chynna's acting had been in the movie and how the director had been amazed by her transformation. He thought back to Chynna's poor dancing in rehearsals and her lack of willingness to put on skimpy costumes. Anger began to boil inside Lucas.

It's true!

Chynna, no, Kenya, had been lying to him the entire time. She'd led him to believe she was her sister when she was an impostor. It explained all the irregularities in Chynna's behavior. But why? *Why would Chynna want to trade places with her twin? And why on God's green earth would Kenya agree to such a thing?* But the real issue was that it didn't change how he felt inside. He had real feelings for this woman. He couldn't turn his feelings on and off on a dime like apparently Kenya could. *Is that why she's been pulling away from me the last few days, because she knew the end was near?* He knew he meant something to her. He'd *felt* it. Of that he was sure. *So after everything we've shared, why hadn't she trusted me enough to tell me the truth?*

"DEACON, I NEED YOU," Chynna said into the phone.

"Oh, really," her manager said with disbelief from the other end. He'd been flabbergasted like the rest of America to find out moments ago that Chynna had lied to everyone including him. She and her sister had concocted an elaborate plan to deceive them all, and they'd been damned good at.

"I know you're upset with me," Chynna said, "and you have every right to be, and I promise I will explain everything to you when I get back."

"And when might that be?"

"I chartered a private plan, and I'll be landing at LA in a couple of hours."

"And I take it you need security?" he asked.

"That's a given," she responded. "But I need something else."

"Really, Chynna? You are really testing the limits here and asking a whole lot of someone you just lied to for the last month."

"I'll make it up to you, Deacon. In the meantime, I need you to get my sister to my house until I get back. When I get there, we'll figure something out."

"Oh, you mean Kenya, the woman who's been imitating you the last month?"

"Deacon, please," Chynna pleaded. "She doesn't have the means I have at my disposal, and she's all alone. She's only got me. And of course, now you. *Help* her."

Deacon sighed. "Alright, where is she?"

Chynna sighed heavily when she got off the phone with Deacon. Her phone had been ringing incessantly since she'd left the ranch. Caller ID showed it was

Rylee, Eli, Fiona and Kenya again, probably in a state of panic, but no Noah. *Should I be surprised?* She'd left him in the midst of a media blitz to deal with the fallout. She had hoped that by leaving, the press would follow on her heels, and she'd been right. As she glanced through the back window, she could see several vehicles tailing them, but she also knew the press. Several of them would stick around to get the story on her and Noah. They'd want to know what she'd been up to all those weeks. They'd interview everyone in town and try and get to the ranch workers. Luckily, the ranch was private property, so it wouldn't be so easy, but the paparazzi were relentless and they'd look for cracks. Worst of all, she knew they would bring up Noah's deceased wife and probably compare her to Maya.

Chynna covered her face with her hands and began bawling. She'd brought this all on herself because she'd wanted some time away to find herself. But then life had thrown her a loop, and she'd met Noah. She hadn't been looking for it, but she'd fallen in love with him, which is why she hadn't wanted to leave the ranch. She wanted to stay and see if she could find something as real and lasting as his parents. It had been a fool's dream, she knew, but she'd wanted to try nonetheless.

The problem was she'd stayed too long, leaving Kenya to hold up the charade for far too long, causing suspicion, all because she'd wanted too much. But then again, that was her, always looking out for number one, others be damned. You'd think she would have learned a lesson during her stay, but some traits were harder to get rid of.

Chynna could ride the wave and deal with the bad publicity, but the scrutiny would kill Kenya. It had been different when she'd been playing a role as Chynna, but now that *her* life was in the spotlight, it would be much different. Chynna resolved to do everything in her power to make things right for Kenya. Somehow she had to make this up to her sister.

A KNOCKED SOUNDED on the ladies room door. "Kenya?" a male voice that she remembered called out her name.

Kenya walked out of the lounge and opened the restroom doors to see Deacon's and Chynna's bodyguards standing outside waiting for her.

"C'mon," He said, touching her arm. "We'll get you out of here."

They rushed her through the lobby past several onlookers until they came outside. Kenya could see the blur of camera lights waiting for her and paused. She'd never been personally on the receiving end of the press, and she wasn't relishing the thought of becoming tomorrow's gossip.

"I've got you," Deacon whispered in her ear. "I promised Chynna."

His words of reassurance helped alleviate Kenya's fears, and with the bodyguard in front of her, Deacon helped usher her into a Jeep away from the crowd of reporters camped at the front door, and they zoomed away from the valet area.

Kenya turned to Deacon at her side. "Thank you, Deacon. You don't owe me anything after I lied to you the last month."

Deacon smiled. "No, but Chynna's my girl, and I will protect her always." Eli had been blowing up his phone in the last thirty minutes wanting to know how come Deacon hadn't realized the truth and how could he have let this happen. That's when he'd politely reminded him that he didn't work for R&K Records. He worked for Chynna.

Kenya smiled. She was thankful to have his help. *Why hadn't I realized before that Deacon is always on*

Chynna's side? She could have confided in him and had someone to lean on during this whole experience. "So where are we going now?"

"Back to the mansion," Deacon answered. "Chynna will meet us there after her plane lands."

Kenya nodded thoughtfully as she looked out over the landscape. It was amazing how things could change on a dime. Earlier that morning, she'd been looking forward to going back to her life of obscurity in New York. Now that would be impossible, not with the hell the press was about to rain down on her. And Lucas, well she could only imagine how furious he was with her and Chynna. Her most of all, because they'd shared something special and what had she done? She'd lied to him. Every time they were together had been a lie.

"Thinking about Lucas?" Deacon asked, reading her mind.

"Am I that obvious?" Kenya asked, turning to glance at him.

Deacon nodded. "You fell for him quick and he for you even though I warned you to be careful. Of course, you're thinking about him and perhaps wondering if there's any chance with him?"

Kenya shook her head. "There's not."

"You don't know that," Deacon replied.

"I do. I lied to him for a month. He thinks he fell for Chynna, and he got me instead. He must be awfully disappointed." She laughed derisively.

"Don't do that," Deacon patted her thigh. "You're pretty amazing too, Miss Kenya James."

Kenya's brow furrowed. "What do you mean?"

"Not many people could pull off imitating their sister, a Multi-Platinum singer, and convince not only her inner circle of managers, publicists and record label, but you fooled the fans. They believed you were her. You were damn impressive!"

Kenya laughed. "Thank you, Deacon, though I doubt they'll appreciate my efforts. I'm sure I'll be roasted in the media."

"Until the next news cycle and celebrity train wreck comes," he replied. "You saw what happened with Chynna before."

"But this is ten times worse than a supposed affair with Blake."

Deacon shrugged. "Maybe. Maybe not. But the two of you will ride it out. And you'll have my help when you do it."

"You mean that?"

"Absolutely kid," Deacon said, reaching across to grab Kenya's hand and give her a gentle squeeze. "Matter of fact, I'm surprised I didn't see it before. You tried to have Chynna's hard edges, but your soft side came through every time."

LUCAS BURST through Eli's door later that afternoon with fury in his eyes. Eli was sitting behind his desk, looking calm and a little too collected for Lucas's liking. "Did you know about this?" he asked his longtime friend and business partner.

Eli sat up in his chair. "Know about Chynna? Of course, I didn't, but I warned you that something wasn't right about that girl. And look what happened— I was on the money."

Lucas glared at Eli. "Are you really going to say I told you so after the hot water we're in thanks to those two?"

Eli shrugged and smiled. "Well, I guess now isn't the right time."

"We need damage control. Where in the hell is Fiona?"

"She's on the phone keeping the media at bay until

we come up with a plausible explanation about why this happened. I was thinking we could say Chynna was overcome with physical exhaustion and had a mental breakdown of sorts. What do you think?"

"Mental breakdown? Are you kidding me?" Lucas asked. "How about the plain ole' truth?"

"And what might that be?" Eli replied sarcastically.

Lucas could see that he was humoring him, but he didn't care. He had it up to here with all the lies and deception. He should have listened to his first instincts and stayed out of show business, but Eli had wanted it so bad, had been so convincing, that Lucas had forgone his better judgment in favor of helping a friend.

"The truth is that Chynna got tired of being Chynna James and wanted a change of scenery. Enter her desperate twin," Lucas said. "The entertainment shows are already reporting that she's an actress on a low-rate television show."

"Wow!" Eli was surprised by Lucas' harsh tone. He'd never seen his boy this upset, and he hated that he was the cause of it, but what was done was done. So he let Lucas continue his tirade.

"The two women meet at the spa and decide to trade places, figuring no one would be the wiser. And you know what," he said, laughing derisively, "They were right. None of us saw it, most of all me. And I," he said, pointing to his chest, "was the person sleeping with her." He paced the room in frustration. "Do you have any idea what an idiot I must look like? She made a fool of me. They both did."

Eli nodded. "We can fix this."

"How?"

"I don't have it all figured out yet, but we'll fix your image and Chynna's simultaneously. We grew up in South Central, and we're fighters and we always come out on top, remember?" He tapped into Lucas's nostalgia of their shared past.

"Yeah, we are, but not when someone ties your hands," Lucas replied bitterly.

"You need to cool off, man, and let calmer heads prevail."

Now there's a first, Lucas thought, laughing. *Eli telling me not to be a hothead.* Usually the shoe was on the other foot. "I have to go," Lucas said.

"Where are you going?" Eli asked.

"To have my say," Lucas said.

CHAPTER 8

*B*am, Bam. Noah hit the wood with the ax, shattering it into two pieces. He went to the next piece and subsequent ones after it until he had a hefty pile of firewood for the fireplace. Hard manual labor wasn't enough to get his mind off Chynna and the abrupt way she'd left Golden Oaks.

The reporters had tried to follow him into the house, but when he had bellowed at them to get off his property, they took heed. But that hadn't prevented them, however, from setting up camp outside the entrance of the ranch's estate, which was a public road, and as he'd overheard from one of the ranch hands, giving a news report of Chynna's hideout.

A news report? Really? It wasn't like she was some escaped criminal that needed to be hunted down, but that's exactly how they were treating her—like a criminal. Noah had avoided watching the news all day. He was too afraid to see what those vultures had dug up about him and his family. Now he could understand Chynna's reticence in revealing her true whereabouts, but that didn't change the fact that had he not caught her, she would have snuck out without saying goodbye. She told him she wouldn't have, but he wasn't so sure.

He was about to hit another piece when Rylee called out to him, "Noah!"

"What?" He spun around defensively. He was not in the mood to talk to anyone.

"I was just coming to check on you," Rylee said. "You've been out here for a while."

"And your point?"

"We're all worried about you," she said. "And the circus that happened earlier with the press. What happened? Is Chynna coming back?"

"Rylee, I can't answer your questions, because *I* don't know what happened," Noah replied and turned back round to chop another piece of wood.

"Have you spoken to Chynna?"

"Rylee," he said, trying to soften his voice because it wasn't her fault that he was upset. "Listen, I know you mean well, but I don't want to talk, and I don't want any more questions, ya hear? So go back inside and tell everyone to back the hell off, okay?"

Rylee stomped her feet. "Fine, Noah Hart. Stay out here and sulk, but it won't make you feel any better."

He knew she was right, but he needed some alone time with his thoughts before he faced his family and their endless barrage of questions. He had no idea where his future with Chynna lie and until he did, nothing in his life would be the same.

CHYNNA MADE it through the private airport where she'd managed to secure a last-minute flight and avoided the paparazzi that hadn't been able to come near the airstrip. It was late afternoon when she made it to Los Angeles, but the press was waiting for her limousine as she approached her mansion. She'd purposely left her phone off because she couldn't endure the incessant ringing from everyone wanting to know why she'd traded places with her sister.

She glanced out the darkened windows to see dozens of reporters camped outside her home. *Let the spectacle begin*, she thought, as the iron gates of her estate opened. When the limo came to a stop, her bodyguard opened the door for her. "Thank you," she said, smiling up at him.

"Sure thing, Ms. James, glad to have you back," he said, "Though I must say your sister sure was nice."

Chynna smiled at him. She wouldn't expect anything less of Kenya. She always treated others respectfully. Once in the foyer, she called out to anyone who might be listening, "Hello."

Just then, Kenya appeared with Deacon behind her and yelled, "Twinie!"

Chynna rushed forward to greet her with open arms and buried herself in Kenya's hair, an exact replica of her own. They embraced for several moments, eager to hold on to the moment before having to face reality. Eventually, Chynna retreated first. "How are you?" she asked, touching Kenya's cheek.

"I'm okay, thanks to Deacon," Kenya replied, turning to look at Deacon, who'd remained silent during the exchange. "He got me out of the hotel and away from those vipers, but I've been held hostage in this house ever since. I'm afraid to go out there."

Chynna inhaled deeply and nodded. She walked over to Deacon, and her eyes welled because of the loyalty Deacon had shown her. He'd showed her that more than anyone, she could trust him. "Thank you for taking care of my sister." She touched her chest. "It means the world to me. I owe you."

"Come here, kid," Deacon said, pulling her into his arms and into a hug. "Haven't you known since the first day we met that it's been me and you?"

Chynna stepped away. "Sometimes I've gotten caught up in the whirlwind and thought you were against me too."

"Chynna, my darling," Deacon said, "I only want what's best for you. And yes, sometimes I go along with the masses to not make waves, but I will always support you in whatever decision you make."

"I'm glad to hear that, Deacon," Chynna said, "because there's going to be a lot of changes around here. First and foremost, I'm taking my life back. I'm not going to let Eli or anyone else rule my life. From here on out, I make my own decisions, bad or good."

"Was this bad or good for you?" Kenya asked from behind her, "'Cause I sure as hell haven't figured that out yet."

Chynna laughed, trusting Kenya to speak her mind. "Overall, it's been good. I don't regret the last month in Tucson with Noah and his family. And I wish I could figure out how to live in both worlds and maybe I will, but for now, we've got to clean up the mess I've made. Any suggestions?" She glanced in Deacon's direction.

"Give me some time to come up with a strategy. Why don't you two catch up, and I'll be back in the morning," Deacon said, "That'll give you some time to sleep on it. I'll also call Fiona." He held up his hands when Chynna began to protest. "I know you may not always like Fiona's strategy, but she knows how to handle scandal. So perhaps she can give us some ideas and then you can choose which one suits you."

"Okay," Chynna said, "fair enough." She looked over at Kenya. "'Cause my sister and I have a lot to discuss."

"See you tomorrow," Deacon said as he left the front door.

"How about a smoothie?" Kenya asked and headed toward the kitchen.

"A smoothie?" Chynna was still rooted in the same

spot. She couldn't remember Kenya ever being health conscious.

Kenya glanced behind her and waved her forward. "Don't act so surprised. I had to get used to them once your people put me on a diet."

"They did *what*?" Chynna said, following Kenya into her modern kitchen. She sat on a barstool at the large granite island and watched Kenya remove a gadget from the cupboard. Then she went into her freezer to remove bags of frozen strawberries, peaches, mango, and a cup of ice and returned them to the island. Chynna was shocked at how comfortable Kenya was in her home. She'd rarely come into her own kitchen except to grab a yogurt or bottled water, and she certainly didn't know where everything was.

"Yeah, they told me I was getting fat and had me working with a personal trainer." Kenya dumped several handfuls of frozen strawberries, peaches and mango into the gadget along with the ice and protein powder and closed the top. It began churning the ingredients into a smooth, frothy concoction.

"Omigod!" Chynna's hand went to her mouth. She was horrified, but not necessary surprised. "I'm so sorry."

Kenya shrugged and walked over to the cupboard to remove two glasses. "Doesn't matter. Thanks to them, I'm in the best shape I've ever been in." She poured some of her concoction into each of the cups and then handed one to Chynna.

Chynna took a sip. "Yum, that tastes good. How'd you learn to make smoothies?"

"Trainer."

"So," Chynna said, sipping on her smoothie, "who do you think ratted us out?"

Kenya was quiet for several moments as she drank her smoothie. "If I had to guess, it would be Eli."

"Eli. Why would you think it would be him? He would stand the most to lose by me having bad publicity."

"I don't know, Chynna. There's something about that guy. He rubs me the wrong way."

"I don't know," Chynna said. "It's hard for me to believe that Eli would try and sabotage me."

"Well, he certainly didn't like my attitude when I came back and my unwillingness to bend to his will." Kenya swished her cup around to get the remainder of the smoothie that was stuck to the cup and gulped it down. "Do you know he actually called your ex, Lamar, to pay me a visit?"

"He did what?"

"He contacted Lamar to try to schmooze me. He thought having Lamar would distract me, and he could convince me to do as I'm told."

"Wow! That bastard. Did he really think I was that gullible? I've been over Lamar a long time. He must think very little of me."

"I'm telling you, I don't trust him."

Chynna nodded. "Okay, I hear you. And finding out who leaked my story to the press is high on my priority list, and if I find that's Eli, there will be hell to pay. What else did I miss?"

Kenya shrugged and walked over to rinse her cup out in the stainless steel sink. "Not much. As you know, I filmed the new video for your third single, and performed concerts here in Anaheim and Vegas."

"And the movie?" Chynna asked as she gulped the remainder of her smoothie from the cup.

Kenya smiled broadly. "Has been fantastic. Getting to work with *the* Carter Wright has been one of the crowning achievements of my career."

"I knew you would be fantastic," Chynna said. "Acting just isn't my thing, and the more I tried, the

118

worse I seemed to get. Carter is lucky to have you. So is filming nearly over?" She'd hoped she'd bypassed the whole thing and could move on to the next chapter of her career.

Kenya's hand flew to her mouth. "No, there's a few more scenes. And I, no, I mean you," she pointed to Chynna, "have to film them."

"Oh, Lord!" Fear coursed through Chynna's veins. "There's no way right now I can go to that filming right now. Not with all the heat we have on us."

"Carter is going to be furious," Kenya stated.

"Carter?" Chynna chuckled. "He's the least of our troubles. Eli and Lucas must have hit the roof when they heard the news. Have you spoken to Lucas?"

The mention of Lucas's name sent butterflies swarming in Kenya's belly, but not in the way it once did. This time, it was fear. She hadn't seen Lucas since earlier that morning, when he'd left her room and all had been right with the world.

"Kenya, did you hear me?" Chynna asked, snapping her fingers in front of her sister.

Kenya moved away. "Yes, Yes, I heard you. And no, I have not spoken with him. Have you spoken to Noah?"

"Don't go trying to change the subject. We're talking about you and Lucas right now."

"There is no more me and Lucas," Kenya said. "In case you've forgotten, unlike Noah who knew your true identity, Lucas thought I was *you*. He has no idea who Kenya James is."

"Bullshit. He's been sleeping with you, hasn't he?" Chynna asked boldly. "Then he *knows* you."

"Yes, in the physical sense, but ..."

"BUT WHAT?" Chynna asked. "He must have sensed a change in you, I mean in me, and saw something he

119

liked. Well, that's the real Kenya. He fell in love with Kenya, not me."

"Love?" Kenya responded. "I never said anything about love." Though she may have felt those emotions, she'd never shared them with Chynna. She'd kept those feelings private, because she was too afraid to think them, much less say them aloud.

Chynna frowned. "Didn't you?"

"No, I didn't. I doubt Lucas has those sort of feelings for me. Our relationship was mostly physical, though there were moments that we shared more."

"Wait a sec," Chynna said, coming around to face Kenya. "You just said you doubt Lucas feels that way, but what about you?"

Kenya spun away from Chynna's prying eyes, grabbed Chynna's cup that she'd left on the island and began to wash it in the sink.

"Don't turn away from me, Kenya." Chynna grabbed her arm and forced Kenya to look at her. She stared into Kenya's hazel eyes that mirrored her own and knew the answer. "You're in love with him, aren't you?"

"Chynna, please," Kenya said, turning away. "Please let this be."

"I can't, not when I see you hurting over this. The only reason you didn't tell him the truth was because you were trying to protect *me* and keep my secret, give me more time. And it cost you."

When Kenya turned around, tears were in her eyes and Chynna felt terrible seeing her twin in so much pain. "I wanted to tell him, but I didn't. And there's no coming back from that Chynna."

"You won't know unless you try."

"He won't want to see me."

"You wanna bet?" Lucas asked from behind both women.

Blood drained from Kenya's face, and she turned white when she saw Lucas standing behind Chynna. His hair was unkempt, and his clothes were disshelved. In the short time she'd known him, she'd never seen him look so distraught. *How in God's green earth did he get here?* Deacon had given strict instructions to the guards that no one, *no one*, was allowed entry. This was not going to be good.

LUCAS STOOD GLARING at both women. As he entered the kitchen, he only caught the end of their conversation in which Kenya had lied to her sister and told her she'd wanted to tell him the truth. It was lies. All lies and he was here to confront her. And lucky for him, Chynna had returned, so he would get the opportunity to kill two birds with one stone.

"So here's the dynamic duo," Lucas said, coming further into the kitchen. "Let me give you a hand." He clapped his hands, and the sound of his applause echoed throughout the large kitchen. "The two of you," he said, pointing to Chynna and Kenya, "may have singlehandedly brought down R&K Records, and I must commend you for your efforts."

"Don't be so dramatic, Lucas," Chynna began, but he cut her short.

"Don't you dare condescend to me, Chynna James." Lucas's voice was cold and the look he gave her was murderous. "You're nothing but a spoiled, self-absorbed, narcissistic twit. So you couldn't bare your life anymore as a pop star, huh?"

"Lucas, please," Kenya implored him, but she could see he only saw red and was going to say what he'd come there for.

"Your glamorous world, full of money, cars, clothes, jewels and adoration was just so harsh, was it?" Lucas circled around Chynna. "So you call in your desperate, jealous sister for reinforcement instead?"

Kenya felt the blow as if Lucas had physically hit her. She didn't think she could ever feel pain like that in her life or that Lucas would be the reason why she did, but she felt it all the same. *Is that really what he thought of her—as a wannabe?*

She needn't have worried though, because Chynna jumped to her defense. "How dare you talk about my sister like that! Kenya is a beautiful, talented, amazing woman, and you were damn fortunate to have the privilege of knowing her, let alone going to bed with her."

Lucas turned to Kenya with an angry look, as if surprised that Kenya had shared their intimate moments with Chynna.

Chynna nodded. "Yes, I know you went to bed with my sister because what? You thought she was me, some spoiled, narcissistic twit that you didn't mind taking to bed, but would never have a real relationship with? Oh, yes, Lucas, I know your type. Men like you want to use me for your own selfish gain, but it hurts like a son of a bitch when the shoe is on the other foot, doesn't it?"

Kenya was surprised by Chynna's defense of her, but happy all the same. Normally, she was not at a loss for words or speaking her mind, but she hadn't been prepared for Lucas to unleash his fury on the two of them.

"I didn't use Kenya," Lucas finally said, looking directly at Kenya and then at Chynna.

His voice had softened, and Kenya was thankful for that much, but she was still speechless and rooted to the spot.

"I thought I had misjudged you and that you'd changed. I thought you'd had some type of realization at that spa and decided to change your life. I had no idea that *you* weren't you." He stared at Kenya. "I had no idea that you'd sent Kenya back in your place."

"I had my reasons," Chynna said. "Reasons you may not understand."

"And we're all living with the fallout," Lucas replied.

Kenya found her voice and finally spoke up. "I know what I did—what we did," she said, pointing at Chynna, "was wrong. I should have never lied to you." She watched Chynna slowly back away and out of the room as if sensing the conversation was about to change to something more personal, more imitate.

Lucas turned the full force of his dark eyes on Kenya and glowered at her. She nearly recoiled from the thunder in those depths. "But you did."

Kenya's face flushed with humiliation and anger at herself. "I know. And I can't take it back."

"You made a fool of me, Kenya."

She gulped hard as hot tears spilled down her cheeks. "I'm sorry."

"That's not good enough."

"What do you want from me?"

Lucas's heart ached, but he had to know why she'd thrown away everything they'd shared for this lie. In two seconds flat, he reached her and gripped her upper arms. "Why didn't you tell me, Kenya? You and I both know that Chynna is wrong. Although the sex was phenomenal." His body could attest to that because even now as much as he was angry with her, his body longed for her. "There was more than just sex between us."

Kenya's pulse pounded, and she nodded her head in agreement. Lucas was right. There had been genuine emotion there. For her, it had been love, of that she was sure. She'd fallen in love with Lucas, and her whole world had changed. For him, she wasn't sure exactly, but she did know he cared for her.

Lucas's eyes probed hers, desperate to know the answer. "So why didn't you trust what we had to tell me the truth?"

"I–I ..." Kenya didn't know why she hadn't confided in Lucas. She'd told herself it had been to protect Chynna, but was that really the reason? *What more could there be?*

When she couldn't give him an answer, Lucas slowly eased his grip and released her, stepping away. "My God, Kenya. If you had just believed in us, maybe, just maybe we could have endured this storm, but now ...," he said, shaking his head, "you've ruined everything. So you're right. There's no coming back from this."

He turned on his heel and walked out of the kitchen.

"Lucas," Kenya whispered his name as the pain of heartache clutched her stomach and she doubled over.

CHAPTER 9

*C*hynna was worried about Kenya as she sipped her coffee the following morning. When she'd found her sister on the kitchen floor after Lucas had left last night, she'd been a wreck. Her eyes were puffy, and her face was contorted as if she were in physical pain. She'd never seen Kenya this way. She was used to Kenya being the strong one, used to Kenya making everything okay. Except this time, it was up to her to make the situation better because she was the cause of it.

Chynna had been the one to ask Kenya to imitate her. She'd been the one who'd asked Kenya for more time at Golden Oaks. And for what? Since she'd left, she hadn't so much as heard a peep from Noah Hart. She was still processing the reality that what she'd shared with Noah had been a flight of fantasy, because clearly, she had only been a salve to help Noah heal the wounds of losing Maya. And now that she'd done that, he was free to move on with his life. How else to explain that she'd heard nothing from him since she'd left yesterday? Wasn't he worried about how she'd fared with those reporters chasing after her?

Those questions were going to be left unanswered

because Deacon, Fiona, Penelope and Eli came walking through her kitchen with an entourage of assistants behind them.

Chynna glanced at the stove clock. It read eight am. "It's a little early, isn't it?"

"It's never too early to do damage control," Fiona said, the first to reply.

"And Eli, why are you here?" Chynna asked.

"Why wouldn't I be?" Eli said tersely as he walked toward the table. "You've made a mockery of R&K Records. Hell, of all of us, especially Lucas, with your charade, and I for one want to know how you plan to fix it."

"Easy, Eli," Deacon said, jumping to her defense, but Chynna stood up from the table and touched Deacon's chest.

"Thank you, Deacon, but you don't need to defend me."

"Well someone sure does," Eli replied. "Have you seen the papers?" He threw down several newspapers on the table, most of which had her as either the headline or a sideline. "The press is having a field day with this, not to mention your fans who are blowing up your Facebook and Twitter pages."

Chynna didn't bother glancing down. "I don't need to see them. I know what they are going to say. Chynna has a mental breakdown. Chynna James's career goes up in flames, same as before with the Blake fiasco."

"And it appears you learned nothing from your past mistakes," Eli said, "because you're still as reckless as ever with your brand, a brand *I* helped you create."

"Listen up, Eli," Chynna said, pointing her finger at him, "you may have given me my start, but *you* are not the one out there every night on stage singing and dancing. *I* am the reason R&K Records is a success."

Eli stepped back and looked Chynna up at down,

glaring at her. Clearly, her bad circumstances hadn't changed Chynna's disposition. In fact, she seemed more obstinate that ever, kind of like her sister, Kenya, whom he'd neutralized by sicking the press after her at the Bellagio.

Deacon rushed over and stood between Chynna and Eli before World War III could break out. "Both of you need to calm down," he said. "We all need to work together to figure out the best plan of action."

"I have a plan," Fiona said from behind the trio.

"And what's that?" Chynna asked.

"You need to have a press conference," Fiona replied. "Come clean about everything."

Eli nodded. "I agree. You can tell them that you've had a nervous breakdown and needed some time away, but you're back, better than ever and ready to get back on the stage."

"But that's a lie, Eli," Chynna replied, "and I'm not going to say it. I need to tell them that I was burnt out and took a break, and switching places with my sister may have been ill conceived, but it was necessary."

"But it sounds like you don't regret it," Eli said, "and the press is going to want their pound of flesh. They don't appreciate being gypped." And for that matter, neither did he.

"I'm going to have to agree with Eli on this one," Fiona said. "You have to show remorse."

Chynna shook her head adamantly. "I will apologize to my fans for deceiving them, even though I heard that Kenya's shows were fantastic. But I won't say I regret my time at the ranch." Even though she hadn't heard from Noah, she would never regret her time there. Not only had she met him, but she'd found a great friend in Rylee; heck the entire Hart family. She'd discovered herself again.

"Why can't you just do as you're told?" The words

were out of Eli's mouth before he could think about what he was saying. And when he saw the furious look on Chynna's face, he knew he'd misspoken.

"I bet you're wishing the old Chynna was back," she responded, "the one that did your bidding and did whatever she was told. Well that Chynna has left the building, Eli. I have my own mind and will speak whatever I damn well choose. You got that?"

Eli swallowed and tried to regroup. "I'm sorry, that didn't come out as I intended."

"Oh, yes, it did," Chynna replied. Kenya had told her how Eli had been browbeating her because he thought Chynna was a pushover. She was determined that things were going to change.

"Chynna," Eli said, softly, "I'm on your side here, as we all are." He glanced at Deacon and Fiona, who were on their cell phones setting up the press conference. "I want you to get free of this mess so we can move forward with the tour."

"Speaking of the tour," Chynna said, "I will finish the tour, but after it's over, I'm taking a sabbatical."

"Say what?" Eli's eyes grew large with fear.

"You heard me," Chynna said. "I'm taking a much deserved break."

Eli was momentarily stunned into silence, but Deacon ended his call and asked the burning question, "For how long?"

Chynna shrugged. "I don't know. However long it takes."

Eventually Eli regained his composure long enough to ask, "And the movie? Or have you forgotten about that?"

"Eli's right," her assistant Penelope chimed in. "You are due back on set today at ten am."

"Shit!" Chynna had forgotten about that. But it was time to face the music. She would have to meet with

Carter Wright, and she didn't look forward to it one bit. "I'll go get ready. Penelope, why don't you come with me, and you can walk me through the rest of my schedule." She headed toward the door, but then turned around long enough to say, "In the meantime, Fiona, you set up that press conference."

"I'm on it!" Fiona replied.

As soon as Chynna had left, Eli turned to Deacon. "Does she have any idea the amount of hot water she's in right now?" He was furious with how flippant she was being about her career, her brand. *Does she honestly think I'm going to just let her walk away from it all because she's found a good-looking cowboy and wants to go back to playing house?*

"Chynna's a tough girl," Deacon replied. "Probably tougher than we give her credit for. She'll figure this out."

"But a sabbatical?" Eli paced the floor. "That's lunacy! She's hot right now. She has to strike while the iron is hot. She can't leave when she's on top of the charts."

"If she got there once, she could do it again." Deacon said and walked over to the table to help Fiona with the press conference.

Eli stared at Deacon's back. He couldn't believe Deacon and Chynna's naiveté that it was that easy to get back on top once you weren't in the public eye. He just wasn't going to allow it.

Just then, Chynna's cell phone buzzed on the counter nearby. She must have had it on "silent" thanks to all the phone calls Eli was sure she was receiving.

Eli glanced at the screen. It read "Noah." Eli paused for several seconds. It had to be Noah Hart—the man Chynna had been carrying on with for weeks and the source of his problems. It didn't take him but a moment to grab the phone while Deacon and Fiona were turned with their backs to him, and he answered it as he walked out of the kitchen. He found a quiet spot in the foyer and pressed "Answer." "Hello?"

NOAH WAS surprised when a masculine voice answered Chynna's phone. He hadn't been expecting that. After sleeping on it, he'd finally taken Rylee's advice and called to check on Chynna to see how she was faring. He should have done it yesterday, but his pride had been wounded when she'd been ready to leave him without a word. Having a man answer her cell this early was a bit disconcerting, but there was no way she would have hooked up with a man in one night, not after what they'd shared. "Um . . . may I speak to Chynna?"

"I'm sorry, Ms. James is busy right now."

Noah glanced at his watch. It was fairly early in the morning, and he was certain that if she knew it was him, she would take the call. "Can you tell her it's Noah? Noah Hart?"

"Mr. Hart," Eli said. "Ah, I should have known."

"Excuse me?"

"You're the reason Ms. James is in such hot water. You're the reason the press is camped out at her doorstep."

"I'm sorry if our relationship is causing her any trouble," Noah began, but then cut himself off. Why was he explaining himself to a stranger? "Wait a minute, who is this?"

"This is the owner of her record label," Eli responded curtly, "whom you are costing millions of dollars thanks to her reckless behavior with you."

130

"Reckless, wait just a damn minute. You have no right—"

"I HAVE EVERY RIGHT," Eli said on the other end, "because Chynna has asked that I relay a message to you."

"And what message is that?" Noah asked. He was really starting to get upset by the gall of this man. If he could reach through the phone, he would grab the guy by his shirt collar and throw him against a wall.

"That she wants nothing to do with you."

"What?"

"That's right," Eli said, relishing the words. "Chynna wants nothing more to do with you, said you've caused her enough trouble."

Noah couldn't believe what he was hearing. It didn't make any sense. He was sure Chynna would want to speak with him, would be expecting it. "Well, I would like to hear that from Chynna."

"Are you dumb or dense?" Eli spat. "Or maybe you've fallen off a horse one too many times. Chynna wants nothing to do with you. Don't you get it? It was fun while it lasted, because Chynna's the good-time girl, but your affair was never going to last. Chynna is a mega-superstar with legions of adoring fans, and you're what? A cowboy who owns the ranch? You two couldn't be further from incompatible if you looked the word up in the dictionary."

Noah sat back in the chair holding the phone in his hands. He was flabbergasted by what he'd heard, not just by what the man had said, but because there was a ring of truth to it. "I, I ..."

"Mr. Hart, get this through your thick skull," Eli said. "Chynna is finished with you. Done. Finito. She's moving on with her music and movie career. Best of luck to you."

Seconds later, the phone line went dead. Noah was stunned and held the phone in his hands, staring down at it, perplexed. Was it really over between him and Chynna? Was it that easy for her to go back to her life without a second thought to their relationship? Because it sure hadn't been that way for him. Since she'd left, he hadn't been able to get her out of his mind from the way she smelled to the way she tasted as his tongue had swirled in her mouth or how tight she'd felt when he was buried deep inside her wet heat.

Oh, God, that's when it hit him. He was in love with Chynna James. The realization was like a gut punch because Chynna wanted nothing more to do with him.

ELI SMILED as he ended the call. He'd successfully nipped Chynna's relationship with Noah Hart in the bud, just as he'd done when Lamar had gotten in his way. And now his wayward songstress could focus her energies on what he wanted—her career. Sure, she would hurt in the short-term, but Eli knew that nothing fueled Chynna better than heartache. He would ease off Chynna for now and allow her to do what she wanted, but soon he would have her right back in the palm of his hands.

CHYNNA DIDN'T RELISH the task of facing Carter Wright, the director of her movie. She was sure Carter was furious with her. First, it had been the Blake debacle and now switching places with Kenya. She could only guess that he was fit to be tied, so she girded her loins in preparation for the tongue lashing she knew was sure to come.

His reaction was the exact opposite. Carter knew it was her the moment she walked onto the set at ten am that morning.

"Well, if it isn't the infamous Chynna James," Carter said tritely.

Chynna took a deep breath and walked toward him. "You know who I am? But you didn't before." She'd been ready to explain herself and offer the reason why she'd gone through the charade, but Carter's calm equilibrium threw her off-balance, especially when the director was known for being a hothead.

Carter laughed. "Surprising, isn't it? Because I should have known it the moment Kenya walked into my office and blew me away with her performance after the Blake incident. I should have known it wasn't you."

"Excuse me?" Chynna was taken aback.

"Kenya has a self-confidence and ease in her own skin when she's acting that you've been missing since day one."

Chynna folded her arms across her chest. Carter sure knew how to go for the jugular. There was no reason for him to be mean. "Is that right?"

"That's right, Ms. James. Because you, my dear, just don't have what it takes."

Chynna knew she wasn't a great actress, but his words were hard to hear. "Are, are you firing me?"

"That's exactly what I'm doing," Carter replied. "I've been waiting for you to come so I could do it in person."

"I suppose I owe you this much, so go ahead and humiliate me," Chynna said, glancing around at the people standing nearby that were watching their exchange. She was sure they'd seen the papers and know the situation.

"I don't want to humiliate you, Ms. James," Carter

replied. "I'm sure the press will do a bang-up job of that. What I do want is for you to ensure Kenya gets her butt back on set within the hour."

"What did you say?" Chynna asked as she stared at him in bewilderment.

"You heard me," Carter said. "I'm firing you and keeping Kenya. Because as you and I both know, Kenya is by far the superior actress."

"Y-you want Kenya?"

"That's right," Carter replied. "I don't have her phone number since she's been playing you, or I would have told her myself, so if you wouldn't mind relaying the message." He turned and began walking away.

"Wait." Chynna rushed behind Carter, who was already talking to the director of photography, sound mixer and boom operator. "So that's it? I'm off the movie and Kenya's on?"

Carter glanced around. "That's right, doll. Because that's Hollywood for you—one minute you're in and the next," he said, snapping his fingers, "you're out. Perhaps you should think of that the next time you want a break from your life. Alright, people," he said, clapping his hands, "let's get the first scene set up."

When he saw she hadn't moved, he said, "Chop, chop, Chynna. I need Kenya on set in an hour."

"WHAT DID YOU SAY?" Kenya asked from the guest bedroom of Chynna's home. It was after nine am, and she was still in her pajamas and hadn't gotten out of bed until she'd received Chynna's call on her cell.

"Carter wants you on set," Chynna said on the other end.

"He does?" Kenya didn't understand. "Chynna, this doesn't make any sense. He does know you're back, right? And that I was only acting like you?"

"Carter knows all of it. And you did such a bang-up job of portraying me that Carter is impressed with your acting abilities. He wants you to play Yvette permanently. I'm out. And you're in, kid."

"What?" One of Kenya's hands flew to her mouth in utter shock, surprise and *joy*. Joy that the acclaimed director *wanted* her to play Yvette over her superstar sister.

"It's true, Kenya," Chynna said. "He said what we all know, which is you're a great actress and much more suited for this role than me. He wants you on set in an hour. I've already called Deacon and a car will be at the house in twenty minutes, so you don't have much time to get ready."

"Are you sure about this?" Kenya asked. She knew that this movie was a big deal for Chynna, and as much as she wanted to work with Carter, she didn't want to step on her sister's toes.

"Absolutely!" Chynna said. "This is your time to shine, Kenya. Go knock 'em dead."

Kenya ended the call, threw down the phone and rushed into the bathroom. Was this really happening? Was she really about to star in a major motion picture?

Kenya glanced at herself in a mirror. She was still the same person with hazel eyes and a round face, except she had honey-blond hair. And for the first time in her life, she was finally about to move from behind Chynna's shadow and become the successful woman she'd always known she could be, and it felt amazing. She would have to call her agent, of course, and see if the series couldn't work around her schedule while she finished filming the movie.

After a quick shower and change of clothes, Kenya was ready and walking down the staircase when she ran into her least favorite person: Eli.

"Eli." She nodded curtly at him, eager to get away

from the egomaniac. There was something about him that made her want to go shower afterward.

"Kenya, Kenya," Eli said as she made her way to the foyer.

Kenya rolled her eyes. "What do you want Eli?"

"Where are you off to in such a hurry?" he asked, glancing at her stylish attire, which she'd borrowed from Chynna. Although she wasn't acting like her sister anymore, she didn't have any of her own clothes and didn't want to be caught by the press poorly dressed. She'd dressed in a faux fur belted vest, tank, leggings and thigh-high boots.

"I'm off to the movie set."

Eli's brow furrowed. "What are you talking about? Have you been playing your sister for so long, you've forgotten she's returned?" he asked. "Chynna is playing Yvette."

Kenya smiled smugly. Eli didn't know. Chynna must not have had time to inform him yet. It gave Kenya great pleasure to apprise him of the latest facts. "Not anymore."

The honk of a horn sounded outside. It must be the car Deacon had sent for her, Kenya thought.

"What do you mean *not anymore*?" Eli huffed, folding his arms across his chest.

"Carter fired her!" Kenya responded gleefully. "He wants a more seasoned actress to play the role. Have a nice day now."

Kenya gave him a quick wave before opening the door and walking out into the morning sun.

ELI FUMED from the other side of the door.

Fired! This was not supposed to be happening. Chynna getting fired from the movie was not part of his plan. Sure, he'd wanted a little bad press to teach her and her bitch sister a lesson, but not this. He'd crafted how he intended Chynna's brand to go and starring in a blockbuster movie was number one on his list. He intended to call Carter now and stop this travesty. There was no way he was going to let Chynna's wannabe sister upstage the main act. No way in hell.

CHAPTER 10

ucas awoke bleary-eyed from on the black leather sofa in his office that morning. He'd slept there the night before because when he'd tried to return home the previous evening after his confrontation with the James sisters, the press had been staking out his penthouse. He'd immediately turned his vehicle around and headed for R&K Records' offices. He was sure the press assumed it was late and he would be returning home. They would never assume he would go back to the office at such a late hour. And he'd been right. The offices were quiet when he arrived, with only the janitorial company completing its nightly service.

He'd spent much of the night drinking himself into a stupor thanks to the Malt Scotch he kept in his right-hand drawer for special occasions. He'd consumed all of it, and now he had one helluva hangover. He blamed it on Chynna. No, it was Kenya, Kenya and her lies did him in. She made him look like a fool to the world for not realizing she wasn't the real thing.

Why had he ever believed that Chynna would somehow morph into a confident, outspoken woman who refused to be pushed around, acted like Meryl

Streep and actually sang to disenfranchised children? He must have been out of his mind. Or in lust, he told himself. That was the culprit. He'd been led around by his other head, and now he was the laughing stock of Hollywood. He only had himself to blame for not seeing the truth sooner. Hadn't Eli warned him that something was off with Chynna? But had he listened? No, because he'd so wanted to believe she'd changed that he'd ignored the signs.

Slowly, Lucas rose from the sofa, clutching his head in his hands as he walked over to his wet bar and unscrewed a bottle of water. He took a generous gulp before heading to the restroom inside his office. Once there, he went straight for the medicine cabinet, removed the ibuprofen and took several tablets. He downed them with more water.

When he emerged, Lucas returned to the sofa and began thinking about what would come next, and that's when Eli came bursting through the door.

"You will not believe what that bitch has done!" Eli shouted as he began pacing Lucas's floor.

"What bitch?" Lucas said. "And can you lower your voice?"

Eli glanced over at Lucas, and he must have looked a sight because Eli said, "What the hell happened to you? You look like death warmed over."

"The James sisters happened to me."

"Well, the woman you've entangled yourself with over the last few weeks has just stolen Chynna's thunder."

Lucas sat up straight. He knew exactly who Eli was referring to. "What do you mean?"

"Carter has fired Chynna from the movie and wants Kenya to play the role instead."

Lucas wasn't surprised. Carter was a smart man, and he had to see how talented Kenya was. Lucas had watched her during rehearsals and filming and she was amazing. Hell, she'd fooled all of them into thinking she was Chynna for weeks and if hadn't been for the press finding out, Kenya would have continued to keep the wool over their eyes.

"Why are you so quiet?" Eli asked. "This is a blow to Chynna's brand and our pocketbooks. You must see that."

"Of course, I do, Eli," Lucas sighed. "But perhaps this movie wasn't the right vehicle for Chynna. She was out of her element, and everyone knew it. This part called for a better actress, and let's be honest—Chynna wasn't it."

"Damn, Lucas, are you that sprung on Kenya that you can't see how this hurts R&K?"

Suddenly, Lucas rose from the sofa and grabbed Eli by his shirt collar. "Don't you ever question my commitment to R&K Records," Lucas hissed. "In case you had forgotten, *I* put up the money to start this place."

"And you never let me forget it!" Eli replied, pushing away Lucas's hands and stepping away.

"That's because you're always trying some crazy scheme to get ahead," Lucas said. "You just need to believe in the talent we have and help make them great."

"That's what I've been trying to do."

"By pushing Chynna into a movie career she doesn't want?" Lucas asked.

"Wait a sec here, Lucas," Eli responded. "You were always supposed to be the money behind the scenes, and *I* handle the talent."

"Yeah, well, clearly that arrangement isn't working either," Lucas said. "I've tried to cut you some slack, Eli, but you just don't know when to stop sometimes. You pushed and pushed Chynna until she broke. And what happened? She ran and put her sister in her place."

"Are you saying this is all my fault?" Eli laughed bitterly. "You were the one sleeping with her. Why didn't you realize she wasn't really Chynna?"

Eli had a point, and Lucas didn't have a strong comeback for it. He'd had blinders on. "Okay, okay," Lucas said, throwing his hands up in the air. "You're right. We're both to blame, but that begs the question, how do we get ourselves out of this mess?"

BACK IN TUCSON, Noah sat despondently at the breakfast table. He'd barely touched his food and had just pushed it back and forth across the plate. Eventually, he'd excused himself to go to the stables in search of his Egyptian Arabian. Perhaps a long, hard ride around the ranch would clear his mind and help him forget Chynna.

Noah threw a saddle on the thoroughbred, hopped astride him and took off toward the plains.

Forgetting Chynna would be impossible. Just like Maya, when he hadn't been looking, Chynna had swept in and stolen his heart. He'd tried to resist it, acted like the feelings weren't there, but they'd been there all along, perhaps even from the moment they'd met and he'd seen her lying face down on the steering wheel of that Jeep.

But what was he going to do with a love that was unrequited? Chynna's record label owner had made it pretty clear that Chynna had had her fun and it was on to the next big thing, but he was having a hard time believing that he meant nothing to her. He couldn't believe that the times they'd shared riding with the cattle, rolling up the hay bales or sitting by the pond talking and laughing, meant nothing. Or worse yet, the moments when he'd been deep inside her body and she'd made those soft moans to take her higher, that it had all been a lie. *Was she really just having a little fun?*

"Noah, slow down!"

Noah heard Caleb yelling at him and turned around to see his brother galloping toward him at full speed. Eventually, Noah slowed his pace and allowed Caleb to catch up to him. That's when he realized he'd come pretty close to the cliff of a mountainside.

"What the hell are you doing?" Caleb asked when he reached Noah, pulling on the reins of Noah's horse.

"I needed a ride."

"To the cliff?" Caleb asked, glancing down. "A female isn't a good enough excuse to end it all. They are a dime a dozen."

"I wasn't trying to kill myself if that's what you were insinuating," Noah said testily, giving his brother a sideward glance and snatching away the reins. "I would have stopped."

"If you say so," Caleb replied. "But even you must recognize you've been walking around her despondent since Chynna left."

"Agreed," Noah said, jumping down from the horse. "But I've lived through worse."

"And it nearly killed you," Caleb said, following after him and they tied both horses to a nearby tree. "I don't want to see the same thing happen here."

Concern was etched across his brother's face. "It won't."

"Good, 'cause I won't let it," Caleb replied. "I refuse to let you go through the self-pity you did with Maya."

Noah turned to Caleb at his side. He was surprised by the intensity in his younger brother's voice. Caleb was known for running at the first sign of adversity, so Noah was surprised to hear he would stick around for a while if only to give him grief. "Listen, Caleb. I appreciate you wanting to help, but there's nothing you can do."

"Maybe not," Caleb replied, "But there's something

you can do. You can get on an airplane, and go get your woman!"

"My woman?" Noah laughed derisively, folding his arms across his chest, "wants nothing to do with me."

"Bullshit!"

"It's true," Noah pressed. "There's a reason I've been upset. I tried to reach Chynna to find out how she was doing."

"And?"

"And I was told to go take a hike," Noah responded.

"By Chynna? I find that hard to believe. That girl was crazy about you."

"That's what I thought," Noah said. "But when I called her cell phone, the owner of her label picked up and told me that it was over. That it was fun while it lasted, but Chynna was on to bigger and better things."

"And you believed that?" Caleb asked. "Who's to say that manager didn't have his own agenda? Didn't Chynna say that she'd been having a hard time with her label and had come to Tucson to find her own voice again? Maybe there's more to the story, here, Noah. You can't take what that guy said at face value. You have to go to Chynna and talk this out face-to-face."

Noah stared at Caleb long and hard. He had a point. Why should he take the word of a hired gun over Chynna? He had to speak to the lady herself to know how she truly felt about him. He smiled broadly at Caleb, and Caleb frowned.

"What's so funny?" Caleb asked, his brow furrowed.

"That my little brother would give me such excellent advice," Noah replied.

"I warned you about underestimating me," Caleb said, pointing his index finger at Noah.

"And now I know better," Noah said, throwing his arm around Caleb's shoulder. "But that doesn't mean that I can't take you out," he said as he laughingly wrestled his younger but spry brother to the ground.

"FANTASTIC!" Carter told Kenya later that afternoon after they'd wrapped her scenes for the day and were walking back to her trailer. "I knew I made the right decision insisting to the studio that we keep you."

"Thank you," Kenya said, but then stopped in her tracks. "But can I ask you why you went to bat for me?"

Carter rose slightly, as if surprised by the question. "Because you have talent."

He said it with such conviction that Kenya couldn't help but smile. It was exhilarating hearing such a compliment from the well-respected director.

"Thank you," she said. "I can't imagine it was easy when the studio wanted Chynna."

"I know she's your sister," Carter replied. "So there's no easy way to say this, but to be blunt, she sucked. I knew it and she knew it, which is why she didn't fight me today when I told her she'd been let go. I'd had lesser named actress in mind for the role of Yvette, but I'd been strong-armed to try out your sister, against my better judgment. And now," he said, shrugging,, "once they saw the film on you and given the multiple scandals Chynna has been in, it was easy convincing them to see things my way."

Kenya's mouth turned upward. She doubted it was simple as that. "I'm part of Chynna's latest scandal."

"Very true," Carter replied. "But the interesting thing, the part you played in this scandal, further showed the scope of your talent. You acted as Chynna while simultaneously acting as Yvette. It was nothing short of brilliant, my dear." He patted her shoulder. "I see great things ahead for you."

Kenya nodded her head in agreement because for the first time in her life, so did she.

"ARE you sure you're ready to go out there and face the press," Deacon asked after he entered Chynna's bedroom and found her on the balcony, staring out at her estate. "We can postpone this if you want."

Chynna shook her head but didn't turn to Deacon. She was smarting over the fact that she still hadn't heard from Noah. Yesterday, she'd been angry at first, but as she'd fallen asleep, she'd reminded herself that notoriety was new for Noah, and perhaps he needed some time to process it. She'd hoped he would've called today and all would have been right with the world, but it wasn't. He hadn't called. *Is it that easy for him to forget the few short weeks we had together and the connection we shared?* She sure couldn't forget it, and now she was unsure of what to do next.

"Chynna." Deacon came forward and placed his hands on both her shoulders. "Are you okay?"

She shook her head again and when she turned around to face him, there were tears in her eyes.

"Chynna, what's wrong, baby girl?" He touched her cheek.

Chynna wiped the tears away with the back of her hand. "He hasn't called me, Deacon. I haven't heard one word from Noah since I left the ranch. I know I've lied to him, but once he'd heard my reasons why, I'd thought we'd gotten past it, but— "

"But what?"

"But maybe he hadn't. Maybe he was just using me as a substitute to get over his wife."

"Do you really think that's the case? From what I gathered, I thought he was an above board sort of fella."

Chynna nodded and turned to stare back out over

the grounds. "That's what I thought too, because he made me believe that he was different from all the other men I'd met here in Hollywood. He made me think there were still a few good men left. And now I'm beginning to wonder."

"I know it's tough not knowing where you stand with Mr. Hart," Deacon replied, "but you have bigger fish to fry, my dear. You have fire-breathing dragons outside your mansion gates, waiting for your statement. Now more than ever, you have to be on top of your game."

"You're right," Chynna said, whirling around, wiping away her tears. She was going to have to put her feelings for Noah on the shelf and focus on containing the damage of her tattered image.

"Come on inside," Deacon said, circling his arm around Chynna's shoulders. "We'll get you dressed to meet the press."

Thirty minutes later, after Derrick and Daisy had perfected Chynna's hair and makeup, and Megan had selected an appropriate sleek red pants suit, Chynna was ready to face the music. The only thing missing was Kenya. Chynna nervously paced the floor of her living room and wrung her hands.

She knew Kenya was filming with Carter, but she needed her twin by her side because she knew her and understood finally what it was like to be in her shoes. Chynna wanted, no *needed* Kenya beside her. It wasn't that she couldn't go out there by herself. She'd learned by being a ranch hand for several weeks that she was stronger than even she knew. She just wanted Kenya's moral support.

"We should start getting ready to go outside," Fiona said. "The press is getting restless."

"I can't," Chynna said, shaking her head. "Not until Kenya gets here."

"I know, sweetheart, but we don't know when that will be," Deacon said, "and this really can't wait."

"I'm not going until Kenya arrives."

"Seriously," Eli said from the doorway of the living room, "are you going to blow another opportunity to clean up your image because of your sister?!"

His tone annoyed Chynna. "I don't like your insinuation, Eli," she said as he walked into the room. She noticed that Lucas wasn't with him. "You make it sound like Kenya is the reason I need to clean up my image. *Kenya* didn't create this mess. *I* did. *I* needed to get away from all this," Chynna said, sweeping her arm across the room, "because you all," she continued, pointing to Fiona, Deacon, Penelope and even her stylists, Derrick, Daisy and Megan, "were smothering me. I needed time to breathe, to remember what it was like to have fun. That's why I left. That's why I asked Kenya to switch places with me."

The room was stunned into silence at Chynna's outburst, and just then Kenya walked into the room. "Oh, thank God!" Chynna said, rushing toward Kenya and wrapping her arms around her sister's shoulders.

"What's wrong?" Kenya whispered in her ear as she saw everyone in the room staring at them.

"I'm just so glad you're here," Chynna whispered and pulled away from everyone to stare into her sister's eyes. "Why don't you go freshen up? The media is outside the gates for the press conference I'm having in," Chynna said, glancing down at the Movado watch she wore, "in ten minutes, so you need to hurry and get ready." She pushed Kenya toward the door. "Derrick, Daisy, Megan, can you help Kenya, please?"

The three stylists rushed after Kenya, who'd left the room seconds before.

Having been put in his place, Eli was glaring at

Chynna, but it was Deacon who eventually spoke. "Perhaps given your mood, this conference is a bad idea."

Chynna swallowed and straightened her back. "No, I'm fine. I've said what I had to, and I feel great not keeping it in. So I would advise all of you," she said, pointing to occupants of the room, "to get used to me voicing my opinions. Now, if you'll excuse me, I'm going to go check on Kenya and see how she's progressing."

ELI STARED at Deacon in disbelief. He couldn't believe Chynna had spoken to him in such a manner. Before she'd left for Arizona, she wouldn't have dreamed of talking to him that way. Eli knew who the culprit was behind Chynna's new attitude: Kenya. Kenya was the reason Chynna had become so vocal and thought she could treat him with disrespect. Clearly, Chynna had forgotten *he'd* discovered her.

Eli had happened to be visiting his grandmother in Memphis and had taken her to a mall the day he'd stumbled upon Chynna singing the national anthem at an event. He'd been struggling to start up his record label and knew he couldn't convince Lucas to leave the Fortune 500 job he'd just started without having a sure thing. And when Eli had seen Chynna, he'd seen dollar signs.

She'd only been twenty, and he'd known he could mold her into the image he wanted. And it had been easy. Her mother had been a softie and so excited to see her daughter's rising future that he'd convinced them to sign a long-term contract, guaranteeing him four albums before anyone else had discovered Chynna's talent. It had been a slam dunk and the start of R&K Records. And he wasn't about to let her wannabe actress/sister ruin what had taken him years to build. Oh, no, he wasn't going to stand for it one minute. He was going to have to teach that bitch a lesson, one that would get her far away from Chynna and the hell away from Lucas for that matter.

Since Lucas had fallen for Kenya, Lucas too had started to question Eli's judgment. He could feel the people in his life slipping out of his grasp and that made Eli nervous—very nervous.

KENYA STOOD by Chynna outside the gates of Chynna's mansion and listened as her sister gave a brief statement to an entourage of media outlets. Kenya had never seen so many cameras and lights, and they were all pointed directly on Chynna, or so she thought.

Chynna gave a brief statement that the rumors were true, that she had indeed switched places with Kenya for several weeks for a much needed vacation. Chynna was honest that she had been under a severe amount of stress for years and had never truly recovered or mourned their mother's death, because she'd gone back to work immediately. She apologized to her fans who felt deceived by Kenya giving several concerts in her absence and personally offered refunds to each and every one of them from her own funds. Kenya was proud of Chynna for such a generous offer. She'd thought that was the end of the conference, but it wasn't. The press began firing questions at Kenya.

"Kenya, what's next for you?" one of the reporters shouted.

"We hear Carter Wright has fired your sister and hired you for the role of Yvette. Are the rumors true?"

"Are you and Lucas Kingston really an item? Or did he know about the sham the entire time?"

Kenya turned to Chynna at her side. Neither one of

them had been prepared for the press's interest in Kenya.

But it was Eli who stepped in. "Listen, guys," he said, "this conference is about Chynna." He gave Kenya a cursory glance. "And we'll only be answering questions on our Multi-Platinum artist."

Kenya felt the dagger Eli had thrown at her as if he had stabbed her in the heart. It was obvious the man didn't like her and wanted all the focus on Chynna. And that was just fine with her; she'd never wanted to be in the spotlight long-term. She was supposed to have played Chynna incognito and gone back to her life in New York. How could she have known that her time in LA would change her life?

"C'mon, Eli," one of the reporters said. "Even you must know that this story doesn't end with Chynna. Kenya here infiltrated your ranks without being discovered. If nothing else, she's been touted as the next big thing, and we're all interested."

Several other reporters nodded in agreement. "So, what do you say, Kenya. Care to tell us the real story?"

A reporter jabbed his microphone at Kenya, but Eli blocked his path. "Thank you, everyone, but this conference is concluded. Have a great day."

There was lots of mumbling from the press as the bodyguards escorted Chynna off-stage, but it was Eli that grabbed Kenya's arm and pulled her off the stage. "Let's go," he hissed.

"Don't manhandle me, Eli," Kenya whispered and snatched her arm away as she followed the path Chynna and her bodyguards were walking. "I don't work for you."

Once they were out of earshot and view of the press on the pebbled path back to the mansion, Eli grabbed Kenya again by the arm and spun her around. "You think you're pretty smart, don't you?"

"Excuse me?"

"You convince Chynna to trade places with you to revive your failing career and who benefits from her scandal? You. The press," he said, pointing to the gates, "want to know about you! And worse? You steal her movie role. You're a real piece of work, Kenya James."

"If you touch me one more time," Kenya said, her voice as cold as ice when she spoke, "you're going to lose that hand. And furthermore, I never asked for any of this. If you want to blame someone, blame yourself, Eli, because Chynna was trying to escape you."

"You think you're so smart, huh?" Eli asked. "Well you're not, because you may have won yourself a new career at Chynna's benefit, but you've lost Lucas."

Color drained from Kenya's fair skin at Eli's comment, because he was right. She doubted Lucas would ever forgive her betrayal. The devastation on his face last night had been evident.

Eli must have suspected he'd hit a nerve because he turned the knife deeper. He stepped closer to Kenya, but not too close for fear she'd cause him bodily harm. "Lucas is all about loyalty and trust and you single-handedly killed any feeling Lucas might have for you. So perhaps you should look in the mirror to find the person to blame for that."

Eli turned on his heel and stormed back toward the mansion, leaving Kenya outside reeling from his words.

CHAPTER 11

"$\mathcal{I}$ have a bone to pick with you, Chynna James," a female voice said from the other end of Chynna's cell phone the next day. Chynna had just awoken to hear the phone ringing after she'd stayed up with Kenya the night before, talking about a strategy for her sister's burgeoning career. Kenya was about to turn Hollywood on its ear and she had to strike now. Chynna reached for her phone without looking at the Caller Id.

Chynna was shocked to hear the hostility coming from Rylee Hart's voice. They'd always been friends, so why would she treat her so coldly now? "Rylee, what's wrong? Have I done something to offend you?"

"You mean kicking my brother to the curb after he'd overcome his grief to be with you? You mean that?" Rylee asked. She'd been livid when Noah had confided in her after much coaxing that he'd taken her advice and called Chynna, only to be given the brush-off by her record label owner. Noah had indicated he didn't know what was going on and intended to go to Los Angeles to find out why, but Rylee couldn't resist calling Chynna herself.

"Kick Noah to the curb?" Chynna asked, sitting upright n her bed. "What are you talking about?"

"Noah called you a couple of days ago," Rylee said, "and a man answered your phone. He told him you were done with him, wanted nothing to do with him, that it was fun while it lasted. He's been heartbroken ever since. I've never seen him so upset, since, well since Maya died. Do you have a new man? You sure didn't waste any time tossing my brother aside."

Chynna tried to absorb everything Rylee was throwing at her, but it was too much. *Noah called?* Someone had brushed him off? He was as upset as he'd been when he'd lost Maya? *Could Noah really have the same feelings for me that I have for him?*

The last two days without Noah had been torture. Just a few nights ago, they'd lain in each other's arms after they'd made mad, passionate love and now forty-eight hours later, their whole world had been turned topsy-turvy.

"Rylee, listen," Chynna began, "I had no idea that Noah called me."

"You didn't? Are you sure?"

"Of course I'm sure. I would never kick Noah to the curb. I love him," Chynna blurted out.

"Did you just say you *love* my brother?" Rylee asked.

Chynna was silent for several moments because she'd been just as surprised by her outburst. She hadn't said the words aloud to anyone, even though she'd felt them and her eyes welled with tears. "I, I do," she finally responded. "I love Noah. I think I have since I woke up and found him staring at me with those big brown eyes of his."

Chynna heard Rylee's audible sigh of relief. "Oh, thank God," Rylee replied. "I was beginning to think I had misjudged you, and my gut instincts are usually dead-on. I just knew that you were as crazy about him as he is about you."

"I am crazy about that stubborn brother of yours," Chynna said, smiling through her haze of tears.

"I'm so glad to hear that," Rylee said. She kept mum that Noah was on his way to her so that Chynna would be shocked by his arrival on her doorstep. "But that still begs the question as who would have told Noah that you wanted nothing to do with him and that you'd only been looking for a good time."

"I don't know, Rylee," Chynna answered. "But you can rest assured that I will find out who tried to sabotage my relationship with Noah."

"Good, you give 'em hell," Rylee said. "But you can never tell Noah that I called you. He'd be upset that I was interfering."

"I will find the culprit," Chynna said, "and I promise not to tell Noah." She ended the call with her newfound friend and leaned back against the pillows on her bed. *Who would have told Noah to take a hike?* Deacon certainly knew how she felt about Noah, so it couldn't be him. Who would benefit from her breaking up with Noah? *Who would even have the guts? Eli.*

Hadn't Kenya warned her that she had an uneasy feeling about Eli since her arrival? Hadn't Kenya indicated she suspected Eli could have ratted her out to the press? *Could Kenya be right? Could Eli have orchestrated this entire disaster to get rid of Kenya and get Chynna back home and 'in her place'?* Given Eli's actions and words since she'd gotten back, Chynna was beginning to wonder if Kenya wasn't onto something. *Can Eli really be trusted?*

KENYA NERVOUSLY WRUNG her hands as she sat in the backseat of the limo in front of the Boys and Girls

Club. Thanks to Chynna's generosity and given her newfound fame, she now had a limo and bodyguards at her disposal every day. Eli may have thought he'd squashed the press's interest in her, but he'd been wrong. Kenya's agent had been besieged by requests from the television talk shows to have her on as a guest and from several reputable magazines for *exclusive* interviews on her portrayal of Chynna and her current popularity.

Kenya was as shocked as Eli that the press cared one iota about what she did, but care they did. Just this morning, several black SUVs had followed her to the filming of the movie. Kenya was going to sweep it all under the rug, but Fiona had cautioned her against it. Fiona couldn't represent her due to conflicting interests with Chynna, but she had recommended another well-respected publicist for Kenya to work with.

"You have to capitalize on your fifteen minutes of fame," Fiona had told her that morning.

And she was due to meet with the publicist the next day, but first she had to make amends. After Eli's harsh words yesterday on how Lucas would never forgive her, Kenya had stared at the ceiling all night. She could still remember the hurt look in his eyes that evening in Chynna's kitchen. Terrible regrets washed over her, and she had to try again to get through to him, even if her attempts were futile and she was rebuffed.

After she'd left the Boys and Girls Club on her first visit, she'd made a monetary donation out of her own bank account and had made plans with Althea to return when she was back in LA. Of course, Kenya hadn't known how soon that would be. And although she was back to help, her motives weren't altogether altruistic. Kenya knew the club would be neutral ground to see Lucas. He would never dream of causing a scene between them in front of the children. She'd called ahead and told Althea that she'd like to volunteer. Something good could come out of this mess.

Althea had been surprised by the gesture, but welcomed Kenya's generosity even though she wasn't really Chynna.

Kenya had a pit in her stomach that wouldn't go away, but she had never been one to back away from a fight, and now would be no different. Mustering all of her gumption, Kenya exited the limo, and one of Chynna's muscled bodyguards Darryl was right there beside her, ushering her inside as were several paparazzi who clicked pictures.

"Thank you, Darryl," Kenya said, smiling at the three-hundred-pound former high school football star.

"No problem, Miss Kenya," Darryl said.

Althea was waiting for Kenya when she arrived and immediately put her to work in the four- to six-year-olds' room, where she could read stories to them. Darryl and his counterpart stood outside the door as she sat down cross-legged on the classroom floor with the children.

The kids were so excited by her return, some of them still thought she was Chynna, and she tried to explain to them that she was Chynna's sister, but Kenya doubted they truly understood. She began reading them Dr. Seuss's *Green Eggs and Ham* as they listened with rapt attention. Kenya tried to use different voices for each character and hand motions to engage her young audience. She was so caught up in bringing the characters to life that she didn't see Lucas enter the room.

LUCAS STOOD in the back of the classroom watching Kenya read to the children in the community. He'd been heading back from the basketball courts to talk with the staff when he'd heard two young girls whispering that Chynna James's sister, who'd imitated her for weeks, was back here in the club. Lucas had thought he was hearing things, but when he asked Althea, she confirmed Kenya had contacted her about how she could lend a hand.

"Was that before or after she'd been called out playing her sister?" he asked derisively.

Althea stared back at him, surprised by his harsh tone. "Before."

"Before?" he hadn't expected that answer.

"Oh, yes, Ms. James made a monetary decision after her first visit and had set up another visit."

Lucas's mouth had formed an 'O'. He'd been sure Kenya had come here to see him, but perhaps she was there because she knew the club needed more volunteers?

And so, he'd gone in search of the classroom where Althea said she was with the children. It hadn't been easy getting in either. It had taken some negotiating to get through those muscle-bound bodyguards she had guarding the classroom door. They hadn't believed him when he told them he was Lucas Kingston of R&K Records, but why should they?

He was dressed in jeans and a graphic T-shirt and not in his usual suit attire. Eventually, another club worker had passed by and told them he was in fact Mr. Kingston, and they'd finally allowed him entry.

Now he was standing in the back of the room in awe of Kenya and her acting ability. Even now, when she was just reading a children's book, she had a way of pulling you in and making you believe every word coming out of her mouth. All of the children sat around her eagerly anticipating each word that came out of her beautiful, sensuous mouth—a mouth he'd enjoyed kissing, teasing and nibbling on as they'd gone to new heights together. Kenya had drawn him in deeper and deeper each time he'd been with her, and now he was lost without her. He'd been useless at work the last couple of days, so he'd come here where he could make a difference and where he was still considered important and not a laughingstock.

The truth of the matter was he could get over being the butt of everyone's jokes—he had a tough skin. What he couldn't get over was the fact that she'd lied to his face repeatedly. He didn't expect that she would have told him the truth initially, as they hadn't known each other that well. But that night in Vegas when they'd made love again, he knew that they'd transcended just sex and that he was falling hard. Or at least he'd felt that way.

As if she sensed his tortured thoughts, Kenya looked up at that moment and stared right at him. Lucas's heart turned over in his chest. He wanted to run over to her right now, pull her to her feet and then pick her up and wrap her in his arms and kiss her senseless. He wanted to lose himself in her and forget all the craziness and the lies that stood between them, but he didn't do that. He just stared back at her with longing.

Kenya finished her story and talked with several of the children before eventually making her way over to him.

"Hello there," she said, giving him a hesitant smile.

"Kenya."

"I bet you're surprised to see me," she said with a nervous chuckle.

"I guess I should be," Lucas responded. "Althea tells me you had plans to return since your last visit."

Kenya nodded. "I saw all the great work they were doing here and wanted to give back."

"I'm sure they appreciated your donation."

"I didn't do it to get your attention," she

replied.Lucas held his hands up in defense. "I didn't think that. It was very generous of you. You know how much this place means to me and how it was a place of refuge for me to stay off the streets."

"I do." She looked at him cautiously, optimistically and it killed Lucas that their relationship had come to this.

"Well, I have to get going," Lucas said and turned to walk away. "I have to catch a flight to Dallas for Chynna's next concert and do some damage control."

"Because of me."

"Because of *both* of you," Lucas answered. He'd had some time to think and knew that he couldn't blame this entire fiasco on Kenya. He suspected that she'd jumped in to help Chynna, but also to see what it would be like to walk in her famous sister's shoes.

"May I walk you out?" she asked.

"Sure." He opened the classroom door and allowed Kenya to precede him. Her bodyguards fell a few steps behind them as they walked down the hall.

"I know this might be asking a lot, given everything that's happened between us, but I was hoping with time that you and I ... and I could perhaps st-start over," Kenya said as she walked beside Lucas. "I-I'm really not a bad person, Lucas, once you get to know the *real* me, you know, without all of Chynna's baggage."

Lucas stopped midstride and turned to look at Kenya. She was biting her lip, and he could see tears on her trembling lower eyelids. She tore her gaze from him and looked down at the floor.

He knew how hard it must have been for her to come to him and ask for a second chance "You're nothing like Chynna. I know that, Kenya."

"Wh-wh-why," she said, her voice breaking in misery, "do I hear a *'but'* in there?"

His face was bleak with sorrow when he said, "Because I don't think we can go back, Kenya."

"How can you say that?" She reached out to touch his cheek. She stood so close to him that Lucas could smell the sweetness of her perfume. She smelled both floral and fruity, like roses and pears.

"Don't do this Kenya ..." He stepped backward. Having her so near him was making him weak with need. It was like his body *remembered* her.

"I can, because we could have something good. I know we can make this work if you're just willing to give us a chance."

Slowly and heartbreakingly, he said the words that would their fate. "I can't trust you, and for me, trust is everything."

Kenya was silent and defeated.

"I'm sorry, Kenya. I wish things could be different."

"I understand," she said, speaking calmly with no light in her eyes. Gone were the smiles and tenderness he'd seen earlier with the children. In its place, were sadness, "But I think you're making a mistake, Lucas. We'd just begun to find out what was between us, and I think you're throwing it all away because you were hurt. And I'm sorry I was the cause of that, but I will accept your decision and not bo-bother you again. Da-Darryl," she said, turning backward to her bodyguards, who stood only a few feet away from them to give them privacy, "Ca-can you help me to the car?"

"Absolutely, Miss Kenya." Darryl gave Lucas such a look of disdain as he walked past him that Lucas thought Darryl was going to punch him, but Darryl merely grasped Kenya's arm and led her down the hall, and to Lucas's chagrin, out of his life.

Lucas slumped down against the wall and fell to the floor, clutching his head in his hands.

. . .

"So ARE you ready to resume your tour?" Deacon asked Chynna that night as he watched Megan pack several suitcases for Chynna's next tour stop in Houston.

Chynna shrugged. "I guess."

"Don't sound so excited," Deacon said. "You know your fans are going to be expecting the show of a lifetime because they have *you* back."

"You make it sound like Kenya was a poor substitute," Chynna said. "That's not what I heard. I saw all the reviews on the two shows she gave. They said the shows were phenomenal."

"I know that," Deacon said, pointing to himself. "And you know that," he said, pointing at her. "But you know the press has to blow this out of proportion to make this," he said, using his fingers to make air quotation marks, "'The Return of Chynna James.'"

Chynna laughed. "I guess whatever works and sells tickets." She glanced in Megan's direction as the young woman pulled out several sexy couture dresses from the rack, each more revealing the last. "Megan. I'm trying to tone down the sexy thing and go for a mature look. Can you find less revealing dresses?" She could only imagine what Noah would think of her if he caught sight of her in photos wearing that getup. She hadn't yet heard from him directly, but after her conversation with Rylee, she had hope for the future. But it was hard. She desperately wanted to pick up the phone and hear the husky sound of Noah's voice on the other end. But she also wanted to allow him the time he needed to come to her.

"Earth to Chynna," Deacon said, waving his hand in her face.

"What, what?" She laughed, swatting away his hand. "Is there something on your mind?"

"Actually a few things," Chynna replied.

"Shoot."

"Well, I want to know what you think about Eli. How did he behave while I was gone?"

"Demanding, same as always."

"Nothing else?" Chynna asked. She needed to know if there was any truth to Kenya's gut instinct.

Deacon shrugged. "He and Kenya butted heads, if that's what you're asking. You know how Eli is. He wants things his way, and Kenya gave him hell."

Chynna nodded as she took it all in. "But do you think he would do anything vindictive, you know, to get back at her *or* me?"

Deacon didn't answer for several moments. "Eli's no angel, but harm you? I wouldn't think so. Or at least I would hope not."

"Thanks, Deacon," Chynna replied. She appreciated his input, but she wasn't completely convinced. *Who else wouldn't want me involved with Noah?* And Kenya had been pretty adamant that she thought Eli was behind the press leak. The doubts gave Chynna serious pause.

"Something else is on your mind. Is it Kenya? Perhaps you should invite Kenya on the tour stop with us. Seems like she could use a pick me up."

Chynna nodded. "She did seem a bit subdued, didn't she?" Kenya had returned to the mansion earlier that evening, said hello and had immediately gone to her room and hadn't been seen since.

"Yeah, since she got back from the Boys and Girls Club," Deacon replied. He'd lived with Kenya for a few weeks and could read her moods, much like he could Chynna's.

"But how does the Boys and Girls Club fit in?" Chynna asked.

"Well, according to Darryl, Lucas volunteers there," Deacon said.

"Ah." Chynna understood. "She must have gone

there to talk to him, and clearly it didn't go as she intended. I'm going to go talk to her."

"Good idea," Deacon said. "But you better get some rest tonight, because you haven't been on stage in well over a month, so you need to be ready for tomorrow."

"I'm a consummate professional," Chynna replied, smiling at her concerned manager. "I got this."

She rose from her bed and walked down the hall to one of her many guest suites to Kenya's room. She knocked on the door, and when she didn't hear a sound, she entered.

The room was dark because the shades had been drawn, and all Chynna could see was a lump under the covers.

"Go away," Kenya said from underneath the comforter.

"That's not going to happen, twinie." Chynna came forward to sit down on the bed beside her sister.

"I just want to be alone, okay? I don't ask for much, so can't you just leave me be."

"I would, if I thought it was in your best interest," Chynna said, softly. "But I don't think you need to be alone at a time like this, not when you've lost your first true love."

Kenya lowered the comforter from her head and lifted her head to stare at Chynna. "How did you know?"

Chynna smiled. "I'm your twin. I know you better than you know yourself, and I've never seen you this crazy about a man before. You're in love with Lucas."

Kenya fell back against the pillows again. "And there's the rub, because he doesn't love me back."

"I don't believe that," Chynna said. "The man who stood in my kitchen giving us hell had to be in love with you. How else to explain his reaction to our deception?

164

If you'd meant nothing to him, he would have let it go, but instead he came here to tell you how much you'd hurt him. I believe there's something there, Kenya."

Kenya shook her head in fervent denial. "There's not." Tears began spilling down her sister's cheeks. "I swallowed my pride and went to him today on his turf and asked him for a second chance, and he slammed the door in my face. He told me he could never trust me, so there. It's over. Done. Finished. Eli was right. Lucas will never forgive my betrayal."

"Eli?" Chynna frowned at the mention of his name. She'd been so focused on getting ready for the tour that she'd let her suspicions about Eli slide. "What does he have to do with this?"

"Nothing, it doesn't matter," Kenya said, "because it's over."

"Don't tell me it's nothing. What did Eli say?" Chynna pressed. She had to know if Eli was stirring up more trouble. She suspected he was the man who'd picked up her phone and told Noah she'd had her fill of him, so it wouldn't surprise her if he'd tried to derail Kenya and Lucas's relationship too.

"He told me the truth, which was that Lucas values honesty above all else and wouldn't take me back, amongst other things."

"What other things."

Kenya pushed up the pillows behind her and sat up to face Chynna. "Well ... he sort of insinuated that I was using this scandal to revive my failing career and that I stole the role of Yvette from you."

"That's bullshit!" Chynna jumped from the bed and began pacing the floor. "You did no such thing. *I* came up with the idea of trading places, so any fallout from it is my fault. And as for the movie role, I wasn't cut out to play it to begin with. It should have been given to a

YAHRAH

better actress, and I couldn't be happier that Carter chose you."

"Are you sure about that?" Kenya sat forward on the bed. "You don't blame me? I mean, I have benefitted from all of this, and you're still feeling the heat."

"Kenya," Chynna came back over to the bed and sat beside her, "I've been in the business awhile, and I know the press is fickle. This will blow over, and they'll be on to the next scandal, so I say ride this wave while you can."

Kenya smiled. "I'm so happy that we've gotten closer, Chynna." She reached for her sister's hand. "It really means a lot to me. I've missed our closeness."

Chynna's eyes watered and she squeezed her hand back. "So have I, twinie, so have I."

166

CHAPTER 12

$\mathcal{N}$oah was excited as he sat in the limousine on his way from the Tucson International Airport to Chynna's concert in Houston, Texas. He'd thought long and hard about Caleb's advice and knew he was right. He couldn't accept what some guy on Chynna's phone had told him. He had talk to Chynna directly and find out if she felt as he did, which was that he was head over heels for her. He suspected he knew the answer but wanted to hear it from the lady herself. And just as he'd done with Maya, he had a ring box in his blazer pocket to cement it.

Rylee had gone with him to the jewelry store to help him pick it out. He'd been unsure of exactly what to get or if he was making a mistake by being so forward, but Rylee had surprisingly been one hundred percent behind the idea of springing a proposal on Chynna. Did his little sister know something he didn't? She and Chynna were awfully close. Noah didn't care. He was ready to make Chynna "Mrs. Noah Hart" and the rest of the world be damned. Somehow they would figure out how to make her life as a superstar work with his life on the ranch, because that's what you did when you loved someone. You put in the time to make it work.

And he loved Chynna. He loved her with all his heart, and he was ready to make it official.

Rylee, his spy, had found out the code word he needed to use to the hotel staff in Houston to gain access to Chynna's suite. Thanks to Rylee's snooping, he would arrive before Chynna and would have time to prepare the suite and set the mood with rose petals on the bed, champagne on ice and more.

Chynna would be shocked to find him there, but he'd finally tell her exactly how he felt.

"ARE you sure you don't want to come with me to Houston?" Chynna asked Kenya the next day in the foyer of her mansion. They'd stayed up talking the night before until the wee hours of the morning, and now it was crunch time. Chynna was with Eli, Deacon, Fiona, Penelope, Megan, Derrick and Daisy, and they were getting ready to head to the airport on her private plan for her tour stop in Houston later that evening.

"No, you go on ahead. I just want to stay here alone," Kenya replied. She'd actually gotten out of bed and walked downstairs in her pajamas to send Chynna off, oblivious to the stares of disdain coming from the group.

"But you shouldn't be alone at a time like this," Chynna said, coming forward to grab Kenya's hand. Kenya was still smarting over Lucas's brush-off, and she needed to be with her family, not by herself at the mansion. Chynna's entire entourage was clearing out and would be on the road with her. Kenya would be alone save for her bodyguards.

"Why do you keep bugging the poor woman," Eli asked, jumping in. "It's clear she wants time away from this crowd. I bet you're just dying for some time alone, aren't you, sweetheart?"

Chynna noticed that Kenya rolled her eyes in Eli's direction, and it made her uneasy. If she confronted him about her suspicions, it would only cause a contentious relationship with Eli, and she had one more album to complete for R&K Records. She didn't need the headache, but she also had to keep her wits about her and keep her eye on the crafty producer.

"I'm actually going to have to agree with Eli on this one," Kenya said reluctantly. "I would like the peace and quiet. You go knock 'em dead in Houston, and remind your fans that there is only one Chynna James."

"Was there ever any doubt?" Eli whispered under his breath.

"Okay, okay, I'll go," Chynna replied and squeezed Kenya's shoulder for a quick hug. "But you'll call me later?"

"Absolutely."

ELI MET UP WITH DUKE, one of his former buddies who'd served time in prison at the same dive bar he'd met Lamar a couple of weeks ago. Duke had buffed up and had tons of tattoos and gold teeth. Eli had to take matters into his own hands thanks to little Miss Kenya James. She'd ruined his plans. His intention of leaking to the press that Chynna and Kenya had traded places was to get Chynna under control. He'd hoped that she would need his advice and be willing to do just about anything to get out of this mess.

He'd underestimated Chynna's new resolve. Her time away had brought out her stubborn streak, and she was as bad as Kenya had been when she was playing her. Chynna refused to play by Eli's rules anymore. Eli was sure that if he could just get Kenya away and back to New York, the Chynna he knew would fall into line. He'd already neutralized that cowboy Chynna had thought she might have feelings for by telling the dumb schmuck that he was a fling and she was on to the next man. And he'd believed him. Eli hadn't heard a peep from him, which was music to his ears.

He needed Chynna to focus on this tour and before long, on her fourth album for R&K Records. She didn't need all these distractions from her sister and a new man. So he'd come up with a plan to get rid of her twin. Not permanently, of course, but if he scared her enough, Eli was sure he could push her back East where she belonged.

And lucky for him, Kenya had fallen right into his hands. She was not only staying behind at Chynna's mansion by herself, but he'd overheard her giving her bodyguards the night off. She was out of her mind given that it was still Chynna's house and who knew if some unsuspecting stalker might make their way inside, which is what Eli was counting on everyone believing afterward.

"So you just want me to scare her?" Duke asked. "Not rough her up?"

"That's right," Eli said, nodding. He'd given Duke the address to Chynna's and told him how to bypass the security guards at the front gate and without the bodyguards inside, Kenya would be easy pickings. "I don't want you to harm her, just put the fear of God in her that she doesn't belong in LA and needs to get back on home."

"Oh, trust me. She'll believe me when I'm finished with her."

Eli slid an overstuffed envelope of a hundred dollar bills toward him. "Glad to hear it."

LUCAS GLANCED at his watch as he drove his Ferrari down the highway. He was running behind, and it didn't look good that he would make it to the airport in time to board Chynna's private plane on the flight to Houston. He knew as the owner of R&K Records that he should be there to support Chynna and help jump-start the tour. But truth be told, he wasn't sure he wanted to be there if Kenya wasn't onstage.

He'd never been big on traveling on tour to begin with, but when "Chynna" or Kenya for that matter had come back from Arizona, he'd been taken with her. He'd accompanied her to Anaheim and to Vegas because he'd had to be near her. And now that she wasn't the one singing on his stage, his interest in going on tour had waned. Plus, he suspected his presence might stir up the paparazzi and a renewed interest in his relationship with Kenya.

Kenya. Kenya. He couldn't stop thinking about her. Or how sad she'd been yesterday when he'd told her there would be no second chances. He'd wanted to forgive her, but if he did, he was afraid to find out what came next. He was used to being on his own. He'd spent a lifetime keeping women at a distance from letting anyone in, but Kenya's confidence and warmth had struck a chord with him. A cord he couldn't break.

Suddenly and decisively, Lucas took the nearest exit and did a U-turn to get back on the freeway. He had to go to her. He knew she would be at Chynna's estate because Deacon had texted him that Kenya was staying behind to allow Chynna to shine. He suspected the manager was giving him a hint to get his act together and get Kenya back.

Lucas would go to Kenya and tell her he'd made a mistake and that he wanted to start over. He owed it to her and to himself to see if the bond they'd created in the last few weeks could be made stronger with the truth. He'd chided her for not being honest with him for weeks, when the fact was he hadn't been honest with her at the Boys and Girls Club. The truth was Lucas had fallen in love with her, but he'd been afraid to admit it to her let alone himself.

Lucas just hoped that Kenya would forgive him too for turning his back on love and crushing her spirit when he'd sent her away. Accelerating on the pedals, Lucas prayed it wasn't too late.

THREE HOURS later after she'd left L.A., Chynna was surprised that she was nervous as she rode up in an elevator at the Four Seasons in Houston. She hadn't been onstage in a month, and she was afraid that her fickle fans might boo her off the stage. She'd received a lot of flack in the press for her decision to allow Kenya to go onstage in her place. Some felt that she'd betrayed her fans, while others chalked it up to another Chynna moment and had moved on. She sure hoped that was the case tonight. Otherwise, it would make for a very long tour.

"As soon as we get upstairs," Derrick said in the elevator, "we need to start your hair and makeup. Daisy and I don't have much time."

"We did cut it a little close on this one," Deacon concurred. They'd left LAX late, thanks to Eli's late arrival to the airport. But if anyone could get Chynna looking fabulous in an hour and half before they had to leave for the stadium, it was Derrick.

THE ELEVATOR CHIMED that they'd arrived to the penthouse floor, and they immediately disembarked and headed for Chynna's private suite of rooms. Most of her entourage went to their respective rooms except Deacon, Derrick and Daisy.

Chynna used the key card she'd been given by the

concierge to gain access to her suite and was surprised by the sight that greeted her. Noah.

"Hey, beautiful," Noah said, smiling back at her. Dressed in Levi's and a plaid shirt, he looked out of place amongst the modern furnishings in the room, but Chynna was happy to see him all the same.

Chynna didn't hesitate rushing into his big, strong arms. He caught her and lifted her off her feet as she wrapped her legs around his middle. She kissed him full-on, and it was just as good as she remembered. No, it was better because the time away had reminded her just how much she loved Noah.

"Oh, my," Derrick commented, fanning himself, behind her.

"You've got to be kidding me," Eli said, entering the suite.

It was Deacon who finally came up to them, still wrapped in each other's arms, and coughed. Eventually, Noah lowered her to her feet, and they separated long enough for him to say, "I take it you must be Noah Hart?"

Noah laughed a rich throaty laugh that sent chills through Chynna. "Yes, I am," he said, offering Deacon his hand. "And you?"

"Deacon," Deacon extended his hand. "Pleasure to meet you. I've heard a lot about you."

"And I you," Noah shook Deacon with his free hand while keeping the other around Chynna's waist. "I heard you've taken care of my girl here." Noah squeezed Chynna's shoulders.

Before Deacon could answer, Eli said, "Well, if you're all done with the lovefest, we need to get Chynna ready for her show. In case you didn't know, she has a show in less than two hours."

Chynna narrowed her eyes at Eli until they were slits. "I haven't forgotten, Eli, but if you don't mind, this is my room and I'd like a little privacy. I believe yours is down the hall."

"Chy—," he began, but Deacon cut him off.

"Allow me to show you out, Eli," Deacon said, ushering him out the door. "Chynna will be ready downstairs," he said, glancing at his watch. "In an hour. Isn't that right, Chynna?" He looked over at his client.

Chynna smiled. "Absolutely." She mouthed the words "thank you" to her manager as he closed the door behind him, Eli and Derrick.

Seconds later, it was just the two of them in the room. Noah lifted her off her feet again, walked her over to the couch and placed her bottom down on his lap. "I've missed you," he said, kissing the tip of her nose.

Chynna nodded, looking into his eyes. "And I've missed you. I have to admit after a few days I was beginning to wonder if I'd been wrong about you. But then again, I knew we didn't leave things on the best of terms."

"No, we didn't." Noah looked stern.

"And that was my fault," Chynna acknowledged, touching her chest. "I thought it was better that I leave before I cause you or your family any pain."

"But that wasn't what I wanted."

"I know that now. The look on your face when you thought I was going to leave without saying a word told me I had misjudged the situation."

"I was so upset, I wanted to strangle you," Noah said. "But then once I calmed down and after the press left, I tried to call you."

"And someone told you that I had moved on and it was fun while it lasted?" Chynna finished.

Noah nodded. "And I have to admit, I almost believed them. I almost doubted you and us and all that we'd shared during your weeks at Golden Oaks."

"But you came here anyway?" Chynna asked.

"A little birdie reminded me what I already knew, which was that I couldn't let a voice on the phone decide my future, *our* future. I had to find out for myself if those weeks together meant as much to you as they did to me."

Chynna's eyes watered. "They meant everything to me, Noah. And I really want to talk more, but—"

"But you have to get ready for your concert?" Noah finished.

Chynna nodded. "I do, but I promise after the concert, it's all about you," she said, pointing to Noah, "and me."

"Then go get ready," Noah said, slapping her rear end as she rose to her feet. "I'll be waiting for you when you're done."

Her eyes grew large. "You mean you'll come to the concert with me?"

"Of course I will."

TWO HOURS LATER, Chynna was dressed her in first getup, with full hair and makeup for the evening. She was pacing the floor of her dressing room at Toyota Center and warming her vocals by singing music scales while Noah sat in jeans, a royal blue shirt and a cowboy hat. He looked as handsome as ever even though he looked like he might be more comfortable on top of a horse rather than an indoor arena.

"Are you worried?" Noah asked, watching her closely.

"Is it that obvious?"

Noah nodded. "Just a bit, but you've done this many times before. Why are you nervous now?"

Chynna shrugged and reached for her bottle of water sitting on the dressing room table. "I don't know what it is." She took a swig. "I can't put my finger on it, but I've changed somehow. I'm not the same person I was when I left, and I guess I'm trying to reconcile this new Chynna with the old one."

"You'll figure it out," Noah said.

Deacon poked his head inside the room. "You ready, Chynna? 'Cause you're on, kid."

"Let's do this," Chynna said and started toward the door. She stopped when she got to the doorway and turned around to face Noah. "You coming?"

"Yes, ma'am." He tipped his hat and rushed to follow her into the hall.

As was her tradition, Chynna walked into the semi-circle of dancers, backup singers and band members to say a prayer for a great concert. Having Noah at her first concert was a godsend. She couldn't have asked for a better outcome except maybe having Kenya there. She sure hoped her sister was okay in LA by herself.

KENYA WAS happy for the solace of having Chynna's big house all to herself. It hadn't been easy convincing Darryl and Mark to take a night off, but what was the worst that could happen? Chynna's mansion was Fort Knox with all its security alarms and with guards at the gate. Kenya felt safe and didn't need the two men following her around all night.

After a long, hot soaking bath, Kenya moisturized her skin and dressed comfortably in her favorite silk pajamas from Victoria's Secret. Then she went in search of some dinner in the kitchen. Her options were limited thanks to all the healthy choices her trainer, *Chynna's* trainer, had made her keep in stock.

She really wanted something calorie-laden and comforting that would make her forget all about Lucas Kingston, but there wasn't a tub of ice cream or package of cookies in the vicinity. She settled on a frozen gourmet pizza with spinach, feta and mushroom. She unwrapped the package and slid the pizza on the rack in the convection oven, which looked just as pristine as the day Chynna probably had it installed. She set the timer and waited for the cheese to bubble.

Kenya laughed to herself. Chynna probably didn't even know how to work it. She'd been gifted with the homespun gene, and when they were younger and their mother was working two jobs to put them through singing and acting lessons, it had been Kenya who would cook dinner for her and Chynna.

Kenya had always been the caretaker, which is partially why she'd agreed to switch places with Chynna; the other reason had been purely selfish. She'd wanted to see what it was like to *be* Chynna. She hadn't counted on falling for Lucas. Her attraction to him had completely caught her off-guard. She'd fallen harder for him than she'd ever had for any man.

She'd taken a risk going to the Boys and Girls Club and asking him to start afresh, and it hurt her that he had been unwilling to try again. Lucas only saw things in black and not in shades of gray. In his mind, she'd done something unforgivable, and there was no going back no matter how sorry she was. Kenya would have to make her peace with his decision and move on.

She couldn't stay at Chynna's indefinitely either. She had to find her own place because Fiona was right about one thing: She had to strike while the iron was hot. Her agent's phone had been ringing off the hook, and suddenly Kenya now had offers to read for roles she would never have had the opportunity to try out for if it hadn't been for this experience. So Kenya was going to have to look at the silver lining—she may have lost the first man she'd ever loved, but she was on the road to a great career. Carter's film was Oscar-worthy, and she was doing some of her best work. Who knew—maybe a golden statuette was in her future.

The timer buzzed on the oven, and Kenya was about to pull the pizza out when she heard a noise outside the kitchen window. Kenya caught a glimpse of a shadow and sucked in her breath. *Is there someone out there?* Kenya shook her head. She had to be imagining things, as there was no way anyone could get through those iron gates or past the security guards and their cameras.

Kenya sucked in a breath. She was just skittish. She reminded herself that she hadn't been alone without Chynna's entourage in weeks. That's all it was. Nothing more.

She turned to pull the pizza out of the oven, but when she turned back around, an African-American male with tattoos down his arms and neck, stood several feet in front of her by the patio doors. He was a roughneck and completely out of place in his surroundings.

"Ah!" Startled, Kenya dropped the pizza on the floor. Who was he and how in the hell had he gotten in here past the front gate?

He didn't make a move toward her; he just stared back at her as if he were spellbound. It gave Kenya just enough time to take off running in her socks down the hall. But the slippery marble floor caused her to slide, and she went sprawling across the marble floor in the foyer. She glanced up because the man was advancing toward her. Kenya looked around for the nearest exit as she backed up away from him on the floor, but the front door was several feet away and the living room French doors were even farther.

Kenya couldn't panic now. She had to think calmly, rationally. "Listen, I don't know what you want or what you're on," She said, rising to her feet as she continued to back away, "but there are plenty of valuables in this house. You can have your pick of the place."

"Oh, I intend to do just that," the man said, smiling and revealing a pair of gold teeth that sent chills through Kenya. "Be payment for going out of my way to do a favor."

"A favor?" Kenya didn't understand, and the man didn't respond.

"So you're the twin?" The man was looking at her strangely. He didn't seem to be in a hurry because he was slowly walking toward her. "You look exactly like her."

"So you want my sister?" Kenya managed to eke out, though her stomach was churning. Now this she could understand. Celebrities had stalkers. Is that who this man was? "Well I'm not her. My sister Chynna is at a concert in Houston."

His eyes narrowed. "I know."

"Wh-What?"

"You didn't think I got in here all on my own, did you?" He smirked. "Someone wants you out of the way, and they sent me to make sure that happens."

All color drained from Kenya's face at his realization. He hadn't come looking for Chynna. He'd come for her. But why? Maybe if she could keep him talking long enough she could distract him. "Me? What do you want with me? I'm a nobody." She attempted a laugh, but it sounded shrill against the marble columns of the foyer.

The man began advancing toward her again. "Oh, you're someone." One of his long buffed arms reached out and grabbed Kenya by her hair. "You're someone who needs to take a hike."

"Ah, you're hurting me." Before Kenya could get out another word, he slapped her across the face. The sting burned, and Kenya held her face with one of her hands.

"If you think that was something," the man said, throwing her backward, and Kenya fell back against the adjacent wall and slammed into the accent table crashing the lamp atop it, "then you're in for a real treat."

He advanced toward her, but Kenya knew she had to fight, and she ran down the hall, but she didn't get very far. The man was taller with longer legs and threw himself at her, toppling her to the floor. She screamed and kicked at his face with her feet, but he was not letting up.

Kenya feared for her life. Who could have sent this man after her? Who would have want her run out of town that they would go to this extreme? Those were the last thoughts she remembered before he punched her in the face, and she blacked out.

"She's wonderful, isn't she?" A male voice said from behind Noah. The voice sounded oddly familiar to Noah, like he'd heard it before, but he couldn't place it.

"Yeah, she's great." Noah didn't turn around at the distraction. He wanted to continue watching the woman he loved, sing and prance across the stage in a sexy getup that he would love to take off her.

"Should be pretty clear to you seeing her out there," said the man, "that you're out of your league, and you have no place here."

At that instant, the voice triggered a memory. A memory of Noah calling Chynna and being told she'd moved on and that *this* was the man who'd answered Chynna's cell when Noah had called.

Noah spun around to face him. "You're Eli, right?" he asked.

The man seemed proud that Noah knew who he

was and puffed his chest out in the fancy suit he wore. "That's right. Eli Ross, owner of R&K Records."

"Part owner, right?" Noah's brow furrowed. "You have a partner, don'tcha?"

Eli frowned. Clearly, he didn't like Noah upstaging him.

"He's mainly behind the scenes. *I* run the show."

"And you run Chynna?" Noah asked, focusing a long glare at Eli.

Eli laughed nervously and then patted Noah on the arm. "You know, no one can run our girl."

"Chynna's not *your* girl, Eli. She's mine," Noah stated.

"Does she know that?" Eli returned smugly. "Because Chynna has never been known to stay with any one man for long. She's kind of like a cat in heat, if you know what I mean."

Noah grabbed Eli by the collar and shoved him up against the wall. Several inches taller than he, Noah held him up in the air for several moments until he saw Deacon and two bodyguards walking toward him in a hurry, and he eventually let Eli down.

"Don't you dare talk about my woman like that, or I'll rip you a new one, you got it!" Noah pointed his finger at the man.

Eli however seemed unfazed by Noah's outburst and merely brushed off his lapel. "You, my friend, are a backwoods country cowboy who has no place in Chynna's world as evidenced by your lack of decorum."

"I'll show you decorum." Noah lunged for him, but Deacon and Chynna's bodyguards reached the two men in time and separated them. Otherwise, Noah may have ripped Eli to shreds.

"Noah, please," Deacon whispered. "Chynna is on-stage right now, and she doesn't need the fallout from you getting arrested amongst all her other PR problems."

"Fine," Noah said, shrugging him and the body-guards off. "I won't beat him to a pulp for what he just said about Chynna. But if he knows what's good for him, he'll get out of here."

"You think I'm leaving?" Eli said. "Need I remind you, I run this show."

"Eli, just leave," Deacon said, exasperated. "If Chynna comes off stage during break and sees the two of you going at it, it'll be in no one's best interest. Go cool off in the VIP area."

"Fine," Eli said. "But I warn you my friend," he con-tinued, directing his gaze at Noah. "You have no place in Chynna's world. You stick out like a sore thumb in your cowboy hat and Wranglers." And with that com-ment, the smarmy man walked off.

"You okay?" Deacon asked, glancing up at Noah.

"Yeah, I'm cool, okay?" Noah tried to reassure Chynna's manager. He hadn't intended on making a scene but that Eli guy was trouble with a capital "T". "But I don't like that guy one bit."

"Eli, oh, he'll wear on you."

Noah glanced behind his back. He doubted that was possible. Eli wanted to cause trouble for the two of them. It's why he'd answered Chynna's phone and tried to warn Noah off. Well, he was playing with the wrong cowboy, because Noah didn't back off of a fight. He'd come to Houston with a plan, and he didn't intend on letting some smarmy lothario to come between him and Chynna. He glanced at the stage as Chynna sang a heartfelt ballad. She sang as if she was singing directly *to* him, *for* him. Noah might not fit perfectly in Chyn-na's world, but she fit in his. She was the woman for him, and he intended to make her his.

CHAPTER 13

*L*ucas was surprised when he arrived at Chynna's estate and didn't see any of her bodyguards stationed at the door. Hadn't Kenya said that Chynna had given her a new detail due to her current high profile status? *Where are they?*

Lucas exited his Ferrari and clicked the lock button. He was walking up the driveway when he heard a bloodcurdling scream that sounded an awful lot like ... like Kenya.

Another scream. It *was* Kenya.

Lucas took off running toward the front door and with his shoulder, slammed through it. A man was on top of Kenya, and she was screaming for her life.

He rushed over and grabbed the beefed-up black male by the shirt he was wearing and flung him across the room. He glanced down at Kenya and saw her face was bloodied and bruised and the pajama top she was wearing was gaping open to reveal her bare breasts and the bottoms were in tatters on the floor

Had that son of a bitch been about to rape her? Fury boiled over in him and Lucas spun around to face the man who was cowering against the wall holding his

183

head. In several large strides, Lucas reached him and began pummeling his fists at the man's face.

"Lucas, no!" Kenya cried.

Out of the corner of his eye, he could see Kenya scrambling to her feet as she clutched her pajama shirt and came toward him, but he didn't care. This bastard had been about to harm the woman he loved. Lucas threw another punch and another.

"Lucas, stop." Kenya grabbed at his arm before he jabbed his fist in the man's chin again. "Please, stop," she cried.

Her cries reached him because he began backing away from the man lying in a heap on the floor. Stunned, he turned around to face Kenya, and he saw her through his haze of anger. She had a busted lip, the beginnings of a black eye, and she was bleeding from her forehead.

"Dear God!" He pulled off his jacket, but not before getting a handkerchief, and pushed it against her bleeding forehead. "My God, Kenya, what happened? Where are Darryl and Max?"

"I–I gave them the night off." Tears were flowing down her cheeks. "I–I didn't think ... think I would be in any danger."

Instantly, Lucas reached for her and pulled her into the safety of his arms. "I'm so sorry, baby," he crooned in her ear as he wrapped his jacket around her torn pajamas. "But you're safe now. I'm here, and I'm calling the authorities."

He stepped away momentarily so he could reach inside his pants pocket and pull out his cell phone.

Ten minutes later, Lucas heard the sirens of the police approaching. The man he'd beaten damn near to a pulp was passed out, and Lucas was sitting with Kenya on a bench in the foyer. She was clutching his jacket to her chest and shaking uncontrollably. He was doing his best to calm her, but she was a wreck. He'd never seen her so fragile or vulnerable since they'd met. She'd always been so strong and confident except perhaps when she'd asked him for a second chance, but even then she'd been in control. But now, now she was a ball of nerves, and nothing he could say was calming her down.

Lucas couldn't believe the turn of events. He'd come here

tonight to tell Kenya that he was falling in love with her and

wanted to give their relationship a chance. The furthest thing

from his mind had been that she would be in any kind of danger.

But she had been. That man, whoever he was, had been on top of

her about to do God knows what, and if he hadn't gotten there in

time ... Lucas shuddered to think about if he hadn't, and he

didn't have any more time to dwell on it because the police

rushed inside and began asking questions.

Lucas walked them through what occurred while a medic attended to Kenya's injuries. Her attacker was put in handcuffs, read his rights and led to a squad car outside.

"So Ms. James was home alone when the incident occurred?" the detective asked Lucas.

"That's right. But she isn't usually. Usually she has bodyguards, but she gave them the night off."

"And the night they have off, she's suddenly attacked?" said the detective. "Sounds suspicious to me."

"To me too," Lucas confided. "But I haven't been able to get her to tell me much."

"She's in shock right now," the detective said, "but the medics are giving her a mild sedative, which will help her settle her nerves before she's taken to the hospital."

"Hospital?" Kenya must have overhead them speaking nearby, because she said, "I don't want to go to the hospital, Lucas." She looked at him with alarm. "I just want to go upstairs and shower. I just want to forget all about this."

"I'm afraid that's not possible, ma'am," the detective replied. "We're going to need you to come to the hospital so you can be checked out."

"Isn't that what the medics are doing now?" Lucas asked. "Do we have to put her through this? You and I both know that as soon as we go through those gates out there," Lucas said, pointing through the open door, "that the press is going to be all over us."

"I understand your reluctance, Mr. Kingston," the detective said, "but we have to follow the book, given what happened." He lowered his voice, and said, "We're going to need a rape kit on Ms. James."

Lucas's stomach lurched, and he thought he was going to throw up. "Bu-but I got here in time."

The detective's brow rose. "Are you sure about that?"

Lucas turned away and his fist came to his mouth. He prayed he'd gotten there in time. Kenya had told him that he hadn't hurt her, but that's about all she said. Was she still in shock? *Did I get here too late?*

"I know this is very hard to digest," the detective said, slowly spinning Lucas around, "but it is best if we rule it out."

Lucas nodded and walked over to Kenya. "The police are going to need you to go to the hospital, sweetheart."

Kenya began crying. "But I don't want to. I don't want to go out there."

"I will be with you every step of the way," Lucas stated, squeezing her hand. "I promise I won't leave your side."

"Promise?"

"I promise."

As KENYA SAT in the police car on the drive back to Chynna's mansion with Lucas several hours later, she realized this had to be worst and longest night of her life. First, she'd been attacked by a stranger who'd been sent to scare her into leaving town. She'd thought after he'd roughed her up that he would leave, and she would be able to lick her wounds. But after he'd punched her and smacked her around, Kenya had seen a change. She'd seen the moment he realized that no one was coming to save her and that he could do more than just scare her, he could *rape* her.

He'd ripped open the silk pajama shirt she'd been wearing and tore the pants off her legs. The lascivious look in his eyes had told her that she ought to be scared for her life because when he was finished with her, who was to say he would let her live? She'd begun fighting him with her all her life and screaming bloody murder. That's when Lucas must have arrived.

He'd burst into the mansion, threw the guy off her and began beating him to a pulp. If she hadn't stopped him, he might have killed the man. Not that she would have minded that much, but she didn't want Lucas to be a murderer or worse yet, go to jail for defending her. She would never forgive herself if that happened. And so after her pleas, he'd finally stopped punching the guy.

The hours since were the worse she'd ever endured.

The police had insisted she go to the hospital, but first she'd had to get through the media frenzy at the gates of Chynna's estate. They'd all learned she'd been assaulted and wanted answers and snapped pictures of her through the squad car even though Lucas tried to shield her.

Then she'd arrived at the hospital to find two women waiting for her in an exam room. One was a nurse who explained that she would be completing a rape kit and the other was a rape counselor. Kenya had nearly passed out. They thought she'd been raped and was afraid to admit it. And she would have been if Lucas hadn't arrived in time, but he had. But they didn't believe her; going through the rape kit process was awful. Kenya couldn't imagine anything worse, especially if she had been a victim of such a crime. It was demoralizing. She felt ashamed, even though nothing had happened.

When it was all over, she'd exited the exam room to find Lucas waiting in the hallway for her. She'd rushed into his arms, and when she'd made it, she'd found he had tears in his eyes too. They'd held each other for a long time until the detective had finally come over to tell them what she already knew, which was that the rape kit showed no signs of trauma. She'd wanted to go home after such a horrific experience but the detective had insisted they go back to the station because it was better she tell them what transpired while the events were still fresh in her mind. And she did, but it had taken another hour before they'd finally said she could go home.

Now, she and Lucas were finally pulling into the driveway of Lucas's penthouse after they'd played a switcheroo with the press by sending out two officers resembling them out the front door. The press had followed, allowing Lucas and Kenya to leave the precinct in peace. She'd wanted to go back to Chynna's, but Lucas had insisted that she come back to his house, where she would be safe with him. Kenya had been too exhausted to resist.

"Thanks, officer," Lucas said when the squad car pulled into the secure parking area of his complex authorized for residents only.

"No problem," the police officer replied and glanced back at Kenya. "Glad you're okay, miss."

"Thank you," Kenya replied, exiting the vehicle.

The ride up to Lucas's penthouse was fraught with silence. When they made it to the top floor, Lucas unlocked the door and Kenya walked inside. The circumstances of her last visit were far different from tonight. The last time they'd been here, they'd made love for the first time. It had been one of the most magical and exciting nights of her life. How could the situation be so different now?

Click. Click. Kenya turned around suddenly when she heard Lucas deadbolting the door.

Lucas held up his hands. "It's okay, babe. I was just locking the door."

Kenya tried to take a deep breath, but she couldn't. The events of the night had caught up to her and when she tried to catch her breath, all that came out were sobs, sobs that she'd kept inside all night as she'd tried to hold it together.

Lucas was at her side in an instant, wrapping his arms around her and rubbing her back. "It's okay, Kenya. It's okay. You're safe now."

Kenya circled her arms around his waist and hugged him tighter. Eventually, her crying subsided, and she released him long enough to look up at him and say, "I could use a shower."

"Of course," Lucas said. He grasped her delicate

hands in his and led her toward the master bedroom and then the bathroom.

Kenya stared at herself in the mirror. The reflection staring back at her was ghastly. She had a busted lip, a black eye and a massive bruise on her forehead, hidden behind gauze, from when she'd fallen back and hit her head on the hall table when she'd tried to escape. She heard Lucas moving around behind her until he eventually came up behind her. He set a fluffy bath towel and robe on the vanity counter. Then he handed her two of the pain tablets that the hospital had given her for her concussion, along with a glass of water.

Kenya took the tablets and swallowed them down with the water before glancing at Lucas.

He was so tall, dark, handsome and *imposing*, but he'd also been her savior tonight. He'd saved her from being brutally raped, and she wasn't sure how she could ever repay that debt.

Looking at him through the mirror behind her, she just said what was in her heart. "Thank you."

He understood, nodded and squeezed her shoulders. Seconds later, the bathroom was empty, and she was alone.

She emerged thirty minutes later through a cloud of steam. She'd turned the water on as hot as she could take it, and then she'd just stood there as if she could somehow rinse the entire experience away, but she couldn't. It had happened, and she was going to have to deal with it.

"You okay?" Lucas asked as he sat on his bed waiting for her. He'd begun to get worried when she hadn't come out after a time.

Kenya nodded. "As good as can be expected I guess." She noticed that he too had showered and changed and was wearing pajamas. He sat upright with pillows bunched up behind him. Kenya felt self-conscious in her robe, because she was wearing nothing on underneath. She stood shifting from foot to foot, unsure of what to do.

Lucas moved the comforter aside next to him and beckoned her forward. "C'mon, come to bed."

Kenya didn't hesitate for a second because the one thing she had learned tonight was that she could trust Lucas. She walked over to his king-sized bed and slid beside him in her robe. She didn't get too close, but laid her head on the pillow next to his. Her pounding head was starting to subside thanks to the powerful pain meds they'd given her. All she wanted to do now was sleep and forget about the night's events.

Lucas turned off the lamp on the nightstand, plunging the room into darkness. Kenya's heart lurched forward momentarily, but then she felt Lucas's muscled arms lightly circle around her, and she relaxed. Lucas was beside her, and she was safe.

That's when the question hit her: Why had Lucas been at Chynna's mansion earlier that evening and not in Houston at the concert? Had he come back for her? The pain meds were working their magic, and Kenya couldn't roll over to ask Lucas the question on her mind because blissful sleep beckoned her.

"WHAT DID you think of the show?" Chynna asked Noah when she came off stage. She accepted the towel he handed her to wipe the perspiration off her face. It had been a good show. For the first time in a long time, she'd remembered the enjoyment she'd always had singing onstage to her fans. The dance and stage production she could do without. If it was her choice, she would be out there with a guitarist and maybe a saxophonist, but in this day and age, singers were expected to give a performance, to create a memorable event. Chynna had done that tonight.

"You did wonderful," Noah said, kissing her sweaty forehead as he walked with her back to her dressing room.

"Just wonderful?" she asked, beaming up at him. She was so excited to have him on her turf, she could nearly burst.

When fans asked for an autograph backstage or requested a picture, Chynna didn't feel as exasperated as she'd had a month ago. Instead she happily took photos and signed her name. The time away had done her good.

"You were phenomenal," Noah gushed. "Best show I've ever seen."

Chynna laughed. She doubted he'd seen that many, but she appreciated him stroking her ego.

"Great job, baby girl," Deacon said, opening the door to her dressing room. "You're back in the saddle."

Chynna walked inside her dressing room, and Noah followed behind her. "And just wait until you see what comes next," she said, seconds before she closed her door and locked it.

While in Tucson and during her stay at the spa, she'd made music she could be proud of, music like her first album, and she couldn't wait to get into the studio to record them. But that would have to be later—tonight was all about her and Noah.

Noah had already taken a seat on the couch in the dressing room and with his large frame; he nearly took up the whole sectional. Chynna easily slid both her legs on either side of his lap, and Noah wrapped his big strong arms around her. There was a hum of sexual energy in the room, mostly from her. She couldn't wait another minute to kiss this man. She'd gone too long without having his lips and arms around her. She needed him now.

Lowering her head, her mouth brushed his gently, softly at first, reacquainting herself with the feel and curves of his mouth. His lips were warm and inviting, and she pushed them apart so she could slip her tongue inside and lavish him with long strokes of her tongue.

Noah growled. "I've dreamed about this ... about how good it was kissing you."

Then his tongue began dueling with hers for supremacy. Chynna clutched at his shirt, gripping it in her hands as an onslaught of need swept through her. She arched into him, urging him onward, and he rewarded her with a bulge pressed hard in his jeans.

"Noah ...," Chynna moaned. She pulled the plaid shirt he wore free from his jeans, so her hands could delve underneath, and she could feel the chiseled plains of his chest and rippled back. Noah, meanwhile, was roaming his hands over her buttocks as he gripped her more firmly to him.

Chynna's senses were so overloaded that she had no restraint. It wasn't until Noah pulled away that Chynna realized how sex-crazed she was. She would have had sex with him in her dressing room with her entire entourage standing outside listening.

"We need to get back to the room," Noah murmured huskily.

"Hell, yes!"

Slowly, Noah rose to his feet. "You shower, and I'll see you outside. Otherwise, I fear we'll never make it out of this room."

Chynna gave a wicked smile. "You just wait until later."

"Promise?"

"Baby, that's a promise I won't mind keeping."

Nearly an hour later, after Chynna had showered,

she and Noah were making their way back to the Four Seasons. She'd given Deacon, Penelope and Fiona the night off and told them to go get lost until the car came to pick them up the next morning. She wanted the *whole* night with Noah. No interruptions.

When they returned to her suite, the room had been transformed. There were candles everywhere, rose petals on the bed and a bottle of champagne chilling in an ice bucket.

"Did you do all this?" Chynna asked, glancing up at Noah.

He shrugged. "Anything for my woman."

"Is that what I am?" she asked. They hadn't yet made any official commitments.

"If that's what you would like," Noah responded, "because it's what I want."

Chynna walked over to grasp Noah's large masculine hand in her small one, and she kissed it softly. "It's what I want." It's what she'd been waiting to hear.

"Then let's make tonight special," Noah said. He went toward the champagne bucket, but Chynna shook her hand. "I'm kind of thirsty or shall I say *hungry* for something else."

Noah's brow rose. "Is that so?" he said, and before she could answer, he swept her up in his arms and carried her toward the master bedroom. He laid her gently on the bed, but that was all the gentleness he had in store because he must have been as on fire as she because he nearly tore the shirt he wore off his back and tossed it aside. He unfastened the belt buckle of his jeans, unzipped them and tugged them from his long torso. He tossed them aside until he was standing before her wearing just his boxer briefs.

Chynna felt severely overdressed and met his actions by rising to her shins and unzipping the velour jacket of the two- piece set she'd thrown on after the concert. She saw his eyes widen in surprise when he found she was wearing a sexy lace teddy underneath. At the last minute on her way to the concert, she'd thrown in the hot little number for later.

"You sexy thing," Noah said as she slid from the bed, so she could slide the velour pants down her legs.

The look of hunger on Noah's face as she slid backward on the bed beckoning him with her index finger could have melted ice. Chynna was sure hoping Noah would help cool the burning flames she had within.

He joined her on the bed and nuzzled the swell of her breasts from the teddy, and she cradled his head in her hands. Noah used the opportunity to familiarize himself again with her breasts by pushing the thin straps of her teddy aside so he could knead and mold them. Chynna let him take control of her breasts—let him suckle her, nibble her between his teeth until she cried out his name.

"Oh, yes, Noah ..."

His hands roamed her derriere and the side of her thighs until he came to the swell of womanhood that beat achingly for him. He unsnapped the teddy, freeing her to his exploratory hands and fingers, fingers that slid inside her to tease her clitoris and make her wet with longing.

"You are so wet," Noah murmured. He continued thrusting his fingers inside her, making her want him even more. But Chynna refused to be a participant on the sidelines. In a bold move, she flipped positions so that she was near his shaft and his face near her womanhood. She reached for the waistband of his briefs and relieved him of the dreaded material. Then she stroked his erection, skimming her fingers along the head. She stroked him faster, gripped him tighter and then she lowered her head and took him in her mouth.

Noah groaned and fell backward on the bed as

Chynna made love to him with her mouth. She bobbed her head up and down in a steadying rhythm, and she thought Noah might become undone, but instead he turned the tables. He gripped her thighs and pulled her forward toward his mouth then slid his tongue *inside* her. The moist softness of his tongue as he eased in and out sped up the strokes, varying the tempo each time, causing pressure to build inside Chynna. When his tongue sucked gently on her clitoris and he flicked his tongue over it from side to side, Chynna's legs began to shake.

"Not yet, my love. I want you to come when I'm inside you." Noah flipped Chynna over to her back and with her teddy around her waist, surged inside her. Chynna arched her back and rose up to meet his thrust so he could penetrate her even deeper. She felt every silken ridge as he filled her completely. Their rhythm and movement seemed to flow from one beat to another without any orchestrated effort.

Soon, they were coasting toward completion, and after one final thrust, Noah gave a shout of satisfaction, and Chynna met him orgasm for orgasm. Spiraling sensations of ecstasy swarmed her for every angle as her body milked his and the spasm overtook her. Noah collapsed on top of her, his breathing rapid. Eventually he rolled to his side taking Chynna with him. He brushed back her sweat-dampened hair so he could look at her face. "I love you, Chynna."

Chynna stared back at him and allowed the love she'd felt for him shine through. Her eyes glazed with tears when she said, "I love you too."

THE NEXT MORNING, Noah awoke giddy with excitement. He and Chynna were finally together again. Last night when they'd made love, they'd enjoyed more than just each other's bodies; they'd shared a deep sense of mutual trust that couldn't be broken despite Eli's attempts otherwise. Noah had finally told her he loved her—and more importantly, she'd said it back. Chynna loved him as much as he loved her. Noah was on top of the world. If anyone had told him a couple of months ago that he would find the next love of his life, he would have told them they were crazy. There had only been and would always be one woman for him—Maya. He'd been wrong.

He, like everyone else, had been foolish to believe that you could only have one soul mate. *Who would have known that I could have more than one great love? How could I be so lucky to have found love again, found Chynna?*

Quietly, he slid out of bed and called for room service. He intended to pop the question this morning. He saw no need to wait. He, more than anyone, knew that tomorrow was not promised, and he had to seize the moment. He would plop the ring in her champagne glass this morning with breakfast.

Marriage to Chynna wouldn't be easy, Noah knew that. They were going to both have to learn how to compromise. He would have to get used to the Hollywood scene, and Chynna would have to divide her time at the ranch with him. They were an unlikely couple, but Noah believed they could make it work because they loved each other. They would convince the naysayers who thought they weren't meant to be.

Ten minutes later, the arrangements were made and Noah was about to slide back into bed with the sleeping beauty when Chynna walked into the living room in her birthday suit, rubbing sleep from her eyes.

"When I woke up and you weren't there, I came to find you," she murmured sleepily.

Noah grinned. "Wearing nothing? What if we had guests?"

Chynna laughed. "Then I guess they were going to get an eyeful." She walked over to him and slipped into his arms.

Noah gave her a greedy kiss and smacked her on the bottom.

"Oh!"

"Breakfast is on its way up. How about we go shower before it arrives?"

She glanced up at him with a devilish gleam in her eye. "Now that sounds like a mighty fine idea."

Noah emerged fifteen minutes later from the bathroom in a robe, thanks to the incessant knocking at the door. It had to be room service.

Noah opened the door with a flourish and was greeted by an annoyed room attendant. "I've been knocking for five minutes,"

The man said as he slid the cart into the suite.

"Sorry about that," Noah said, following him into the living room. "I was in the shower and didn't hear the door."

Chynna joined them in the living room wearing a matching robe, and the attendant glanced back at Noah. "Now I know why you didn't hear the door." The attendant smiled.

"Don't you worry about that," Noah said, sliding him a twenty dollar bill from his wallet.

"Thank you, sir." The attendant nodded then bowed before heading toward the door.

"He was cheeky, wasn't he?" Chynna said, walking to the cart and opening the lid on the plates. She grabbed a slice of bacon and began munching.

"Guess we were having a lot of fun bathing," Noah responded with a wink.

"We wanted to get really clean," Chynna said, plopping down on the sofa. She reached for the remote to turn on the television.

Noah was disappointed. He didn't envision proposing to her with the television in the background. "Babe, I was hoping we could have," Noah began, but before he could finish saying "a romantic breakfast," he watched the reporter onscreen announce that Kenya James, sister of Chynna James, had been assaulted in Chynna's mansion the previous evening.

"Omigod, Noah!" Chynna screamed and covered her mouth with her hands.

Noah rushed to her side on the couch. They listened to the reports, which indicated that Kenya had been alone when an unknown intruder assaulted her in her sister's home. Images flashed of Kenya and then of Lucas Kingston, who'd reportedly heard her screaming and rushed in to save her. An arrest was made and an investigation was underway.

Using the remote, Chynna turned off the television. "How the hell could something like this have happened? I have top of the line security at the mansion. Do you think Kenya was, was raped?"

"I don't know, babe." Noah sure hoped not. He wouldn't wish such a horrific act on any woman, and he prayed Chynna's sister was not a victim.

"And why didn't anyone call me?" she said.

"Remember we sort of turned our cell phones off in the limo," Noah replied.

"That's right. I have to call my sister *now*." Chynna glanced around the living room for her phone. She jumped up when she saw it on the settee nearby and immediately began dialing Kenya's cell phone. Her call went right to voicemail.

"She's not answering," Chynna said. Alarm was written across her fair features. "I need to get home." She began rushing toward the bedroom. "I have to get to my sister."

"Of course, of course," Noah said, rising and following her. "What can I do?"

Chynna scratched her head. "I'm calling Deacon." She placed her cell phone to her ear. "I need to get my plane up in the air in an hour. Kenya needs me."

CHAPTER 14

*L*ucas did not relish taking Kenya back to the scene of a crime where she was so viciously attacked, but Kenya had insisted on returning. He'd only agreed after insisting she eat the breakfast he'd made of eggs, bacon, toast and fresh fruit. She'd attempted a few bites but hadn't each much on the plate before he'd finally agreed to do as she asked.

"I have to go back," Kenya explained as they drove to Chynna's estate. "This story is out there, and Chynna's got to have seen it. I left my cell phone at the house, and Chynna's bound to be worried. We have to get back."

"Okay, okay," Lucas said. He didn't want Kenya getting overly excited. She'd been through enough right now, which is why he was going to have to wait to tell her how he truly felt. Last night had shown him he had not just fallen for her, but was *in love* with her. He didn't see his life without her in it. He couldn't tell her that now because she wouldn't believe him. What was that saying about how people say things after a traumatic experience? His change of heart had nothing to do with the thought of nearly losing her last night, though he would have lost his mind had that happened.

He'd realized on his way to the airport that he wanted her in his life, and he needed Kenya to believe it when he told her.

They arrived at the mansion to find the entire house in order. The police tape was gone and the damaged furniture had been removed. It was as if nothing had ever happened, though Lucas doubted Kenya would ever forget it.

"You okay?" he asked, squeezing her hand as she looked around the foyer.

Kenya nodded, but she didn't speak. She released his hand and began walking down the hall. He didn't know if she was remembering the events of the night before, so he just followed behind her. He wanted to be her anchor. He wanted her to know he wasn't going anywhere.

She made it to the kitchen and stood looking at the room and a frown came across her face.

"What's wrong?" Lucas asked. "Do you remember something?"

Kenya nodded.

"Something bad."

She nodded again.

Kenya was about to speak when she heard Chynna's voice: "Kenya, Kenya, where are you?"

Kenya glanced toward the door and took off running, leaving Lucas to wonder exactly what it was she had been about to say.

CHYNNA FELL SLIGHTLY BACKWARD, and Noah had to catch her when Kenya came running toward them. She was shocked to see her sister so badly beaten. "Oh, thank God," Chynna said when Kenya rushed into her arms and they embraced. "Thank God, you're alright."

"I wouldn't say alright," Lucas said from behind

Kenya. "But she's in one piece." Lucas must have noticed Noah standing behind her because he offered him his hand. "Lucas Kingston."

"Noah Hart."

Lucas smiled knowingly. "Ah, so you're Noah."

"I guess my reputation precedes me," Noah replied.

"Something like that," Lucas said.

"Let me look at you," Chynna said, stepping back and surveying Kenya, lightly touching her bruised cheek. "Any broken bones?"

Kenya shook her head. "No, but I had a slight concussion. I'll have to go back and get checked later."

"You'll do no such thing," Chynna said, wrapping her arm around Kenya and leading her to the living room. "We'll bring a doctor here. You've been through enough."

Both men followed the women into the living room adjacent to the foyer.

Chynna sat down with Kenya on one of the sofas. "Can you tell me what happened? Why weren't Darryl and Max here?"

Kenya inhaled deeply. "I told them to take the night off. I thought it would be o-okay," she said, her voice breaking. "But it wasn't ... I saw a shadow outside and before I knew it, he was inside the house."

Chynna squeezed her hand to encourage her to continue.

"He chased me down the hall and caught me in the foyer. I tried to fight him, but he, he hit me," Kenya said, touching her cheek at the remembrance, "threw me to the floor, then he climbed on top of me and—"

"I think that's enough," Lucas said, coming to Kenya's side. He sat next to her on the sofa.

"I'm so sorry," Chynna said, her eyes filling with tears, "that this happened while you were in *my* home."

"It's not your fault," Kenya said, glancing at Chynna.

She could see Chynna was blaming herself what had occurred. "You mustn't blame yourself."

"Isn't it?" Chynna asked. "He was probably some stalker looking for me, and you look just like me ..."

"He wasn't here for you," Kenya said quietly.

"What do you mean?"

"He was here for *me*."

Chynna's forehead wrinkled. She didn't understand. She wasn't sure she wanted too. She could hear the front door opening and voices in the hall as Eli, Deacon, Fiona, Penelope and some of her staff came inside. But she had to focus on Kenya's story.

"He told me he was here to teach me a lesson so I would leave town."

"Why would some random stranger go through the trouble to break in here to scare you into leaving town?"

"Because he wasn't random," Kenya replied. "Someone sent him."

"Who?" Chynna, Lucas and Noah asked almost simultaneously.

"Eli."

ELI WALKED into Chynna's living room with her crew to see all eyes were on him. He saw Kenya first, and she looked terrible. Her right eye was nearly closed shut thanks to a black eye, and she had cuts and contusions all over her face. He'd heard she'd been attacked, but didn't know how bad it was until now. *Could Duke really have done this?*

He glanced in Lucas's direction and the look of absolute hatred on Lucas's face startled him. Eli took a step backward.

"What's going on in here?" He asked, attempting to

sound lighthearted when he felt far from it. There was a distinct air of hostility in the room.

"Kenya!" When Deacon saw her he rushed toward her.

"I don't know, Eli," Lucas said, rising and pacing the floor agitatedly. "Why don't you tell us?"

Eli shrugged. "I don't know what you mean."

"Liar!" Kenya rose to face Eli, pushing past Deacon and Fiona and stalking toward him. "I know what you did."

"What I did?" He touched his chest for dramatic effect. "I just got back from Houston. What could I have done?" The best defense was to feign ignorance.

"You sent that man after me. You sent him here to teach me a lesson, make me want to leave Los Angeles so I wouldn't steal Chynna's thunder," she said, turning to look back at her sister. "But I didn't, so you had to get creative, huh? You sent that bastard to terrorize me."

"That's ridiculous," Eli replied. "And I'm outraged that you would think such a thing. I might not be your biggest fan, but I would never send someone to harm you."

Noah Hart walked toward him. "Like you wouldn't pick up Chynna's cell phone and tell me that Chynna wanted nothing to do with me. You wouldn't lie and tell me that Chynna and I were through and the fun was over?"

Eli glanced at Chynna and instead of appearing horrified by Noah's statement; she was nodding her head in agreement.

"Or how about the fact that you called in Lamar, Chynna's ex-boyfriend, to *handle me*," Kenya said, "because while I played Chynna, I wasn't doing your bidding."

Eli glanced at Chynna. "Surely you can't believe this,

Chynna. You know I've always had your best interest at heart." Then he glanced at Lucas, his best friend of twenty years, and said, "And you, you know I wouldn't do this to you. I know how you feel about Kenya, that you love her. I would never hurt her."

Bull's-eye. Kenya stared at Lucas with a dumb-founded expression on her face. Eli so loved it when he could drop a bomb and watch the fallout. The poor girl was looking at Lucas with questions in her eyes. The downside was Lucas looked like he was ready to rip Eli's heart out.

Chynna was the first to speak and rose from the circle to come forward. "You know what I believe, Eli?" she said. "I believe you are a lying, two-timing, con-niving criminal who set my sister up to be beaten and worse, *raped*." Her voice steadily rose. "I believe you called Noah and told him I didn't want him so you could interfere in our relationship just as you inter-fered with Lamar and me all those years ago."

"I, I—" But she didn't let him finish.

"And I believe," she said, pointing her finger in Eli's face, "that you *knew* Kenya and I switched places. *You* leaked the story to the press and unleashed the pa-parazzi on all of us." On that, she pointed to Kenya, Lucas and Noah.

"Eli leaked the story?" Lucas's dark eyes were again on Eli, and he could feel himself begin to sweat. Ever since they were little kids, he'd always known that there was a switch on Lucas. And if crossed, he would become another man; Eli could see that switch being turned on, and he began backing up toward the door.

"Okay, okay," Eli replied as he made his way to the doorway. "So I leaked the story." He had to get in front of this and admit to half- truths before the situation all went to hell in a handbasket. "I mean bad press is good press, right?" He shrugged, but no one seemed to be buying it. Even Deacon was looking at him with disgust. "And I couldn't let *her*," Eli said, inclining his head toward Kenya, "imitate you. She was nothing but a poor imitation of you." He saw Kenya flinch at his words. Score again!

"You nearly ruined me! "And you almost ...," Chynna said, reaching for Noah's hand, "almost cost me the man I loved."

Fury boiled within Eli, and the posture he'd been working on maintaining for so long finally broke. He said what he really thought. "And whose fault is all of this, Chynna? You've been in one disaster after another. First there was the Blake incident and now all of this. *You* started this whole thing in motion. *We*," he said, pointing to Lucas, "didn't tell you to switch places. *You* got that bright idea all on your own. And how smart was that?"

Eli saw Noah make a move toward him, but he didn't back down. "*You* are the cause of your own drama, baby girl. *You two*," Eli said, pointing to Noah, "were never going to work. Don't you know that love and fame can't exist in the same place? And well," he said, turning to Kenya, "I had no idea Duke would go after you that way."

Eli's hand flew to his mouth at the slip-up. He was standing in front of a room with tons of witnesses. "I, I meant that I would never have dreamed that something this terrible could have happened."

"Bullshit!" Kenya yelled. "You could have gotten me raped, Eli. Or worse, killed!"

Eli didn't know what to do. He was cornered. Everyone was yelling and screaming at him, but the worst was Lucas. The look of disappointment would haunt Eli forever.

. . .

"How could you do this to me, man, after everything we've been through together?" Lucas was choked up. He'd been listening to all the allegations that Kenya, Chynna and even Noah had lodged against Eli. They all couldn't be making it up, it had to be true. The person he'd aligned himself with was a liar and a criminal. Lucas beat his chest and cried out, "You've been my friend for twenty years strong. How could you send some thug after the woman I love?"

Kenya glanced up at him in amazement just as she'd done when Eli had said he loved her, except this time, it had come from him. The timing of telling Kenya this with an audience wasn't how Lucas had envisioned telling her he loved her for the first time, but it was the truth. He was done with all the lies, and Eli's scheming.

"I didn't do it," Eli said. He looked everywhere except Lucas in the eye. Lucas used to be able to discern when Eli was lying and this time, he did. Finally, he could see Eli was not the man he thought he was. He wasn't the same young boy he'd grown up with in South Central. He'd changed. Money and power had changed him.

Lucas lunged for Eli and grabbed him on either side of his collar. He threw him up against the wall.

"Lucas, don't. Let's just call the police and let them deal with this scum," Noah said, trying to grab his arm.

But Lucas jerked him off. "Tell me the truth, Eli," he shouted, holding his arm under Eli's windpipe. "Admit what you did?"

"Why? So you can go back to sleeping with some two-bit wannabe? She'll never be as good as her sister. She used this situation to her advantage and tied her hitch to Chynna's wagon so she'd get famous. She's nothing but a low-rate—"

Eli never got the words out because Lucas punched him in the face, and Eli went sprawling to the floor.

Lucas wanted to beat him to a pulp like he'd done the man last night, but he couldn't, so he turned to walk way. He was going to have to figure out how to extricate himself from this disaster of a partnership.

"So, you're choosing her," Eli said, pointing to Kenya on the couch as he held his jaw on the floor, "over me? Hell, I should have had Duke finish her off."

Lucas turned to lunge at him, but Noah caught him in time before he made a stupid mistake.

Eli rose to his feet and reached inside his suit coat for a handkerchief to hold to his jaw and bleeding lip. "Nothing I've done is criminal," he said.

"Like hell there isn't. You masterminded Kenya's assault!" Chynna responded.

"Try proving it!" Eli shouted.

"I think we have quite a few witnesses in this room that can attest to your confession," Lucas said.

Eli shrugged. "Good luck making it stick." He turned on his heel and walked out the living room. Seconds later, Lucas heard the front door shut.

"Omigod, Kenya," Chynna said, rushing to Kenya's side. Lucas was envious because he wanted to be the person she leaned on right now. "I can't believe Eli sent someone to attack you."

"It explains how the man would have gotten through security or even through the house," Lucas said. "Eli just confessed, and I'm sure that thug is looking for a way out. We'll get him, Kenya. I won't rest until I see Eli brought to justice."

"But what about R&K Records?" Kenya asked.

"I don't care about the company," Lucas said, looking across the room at her. "All I care about is you."

KENYA WAS silent as was the entire room at Lucas's declaration. Her head was reeling. She couldn't believe what had happened in the last twenty-four hours. She had been attacked. Eli had confessed to all his scheming. Lucas had said he loved her. It was all so unreal.

"If you all don't mind, I would like to talk to Lucas alone," she said, pointedly looking at her twin.

Chynna nodded and headed toward the door with Noah following right behind her. If anyone could read her mind and know what she was thinking, it was her twin. She would know that Kenya was long overdue for a talk with the man she loved. And now she knew he felt the same.

After the rest of Chynna's entourage had cleared the room, Kenya repeated back Lucas's sentiment from earlier: "All you care about is me?"

Lucas nodded and walked over to kneel beside her at the couch. "I guess we have a lot talk about."

"Ya think?"

He stared at her for several long moments before saying, "I came here last night to the mansion because I'd had a change of heart. I came here to tell you that I'd fallen for you, and I wanted to try again."

Kenya's heart began pounding loudly in her chest, so much so she thought he could hear it, but he didn't. He just kept talking. She'd been right. He'd had to come back for her.

"But instead I found you being brutally attacked ... and it triggered something that I guess I already knew deep down inside but had been trying to push down, which was that I hadn't just fallen for you, I loved you." He corrected himself: "Love you."

Tears welled in Kenya's eyes. "You love me?" Kenya began to shake uncontrollably. "At the club, when I asked you for a second chance, you threw it back in my face. I,I thought you didn't want me. Do you know how much that hurt?" The sting of his rejection had been tearing her up inside.

Lucas reached for her hand. "I do." He brought her hand to his lips and kissed it. "And I'm sorry I ever told you that I didn't want you because I can't imagine my life without you in it, Kenya. Please tell me that I haven't broken us and that there's still a chance for us?"

"But what about trust and loyalty?" Kenya inquired. "I know those are important qualities and I let you down on both accounts."

"I want all those qualities in my mate," Lucas answered honestly, "But I'm also willing to forgive and let go of the past."

"You will?"

"Yes." Lucas stated emphatically. "I need you, Kenya."

Kenya slapped his shoulder with one of her hands. "Then of course, there's a chance for us, you fool. I never stopped loving you or wanting you."

Lucas pulled Kenya into his arms, grasped both sides of her face and began kissing her all over, from her forehead to her cheek to her lips.

"Ouch!"

"I'm so sorry, babe." He pushed away to look at her. In his haste, he'd momentarily forgotten about her injuries.

Kenya smiled. "It's okay." She lovingly stroked his cheek. "It's okay, it's okay." And for the first time in a long time, Kenya knew it would be. She and Lucas had found their way back to each other, and she looked forward to a long future together.

"CAN YOU BELIEVE, ELI?" Chynna asked Noah as they stood on the balcony outside her bedroom drinking wine. "He set all of this in motion."

"Actually I can," Noah said. "I don't know the guy,

but the instant I met him, I disliked him. And well, the feeling was mutual."

"Did something happen in Houston?"

"Oh, yeah," Noah replied. "That guy pretty much called you a slut and told me you'd sleep with anything in jeans."

Chynna's hand flew to her mouth. "Omigod!"

"I nearly tore him apart backstage, and I would have if Deacon hadn't intervened."

"Why did I never see any of it before?" Chynna asked, sipping her wine. How could she be so naïve not to see that she had a snake in her camp?

"Sometimes when you're really close to a situation, you can't see the forest for the trees."

"True, but Eli's actions weren't just mean-spirited, they turned criminal. How could he send that bastard after my sister?"

"I don't know, Chynna." Noah's cell phone began ringing at his side. He glanced down at the display. It read 'Rylee.' "Excuse me for a minute ... it's Rylee."

"Send her my love," Chynna said as Noah stepped off the balcony and back inside the master bedroom.

"HEY, LITTLE SIS, HOW ARE THINGS?" Noah asked, trying to sound lighthearted when he felt far from it. The events of the day had not only taken their toll on Chynna but on him as well.

"How are things?" Rylee asked from Tucson. "How the heck do you think? We haven't heard from you in over twenty-four hours then the family sees that Chynna's sister was attacked at *her home*. What the hell are we supposed to think? Are you okay? What's going on?" She fired a million questions at him.

"Everything's fine," Noah said. "At least now it is."

"What happened? Details, please," Rylee wanted answers as she wasn't about to take a pat answer.

Noah sat down on Chynna's bed and watched her pace the balcony outside. She had to feel terrible that the owner of her record label had tried to harm her sister all because he wanted control over Chynna. "You want the short story or the long story?"

"How about something in the middle?"

"Well, as you've already seen on the news, Chynna's sister, Kenya, was assaulted by what the news reporters thought was an unknown assailant."

"But?"

"But he wasn't. Turns out he was hired by Eli, one of the owners of Chynna's record label. Eli wanted to run Kenya out of town because he felt she was stealing the spotlight from Chynna. He was also the one who leaked the story about them switching places. And when that didn't work, he took matters into his own hands, by hiring someone to scare Kenya off. Except the thug got overzealous and not only roughed her up, but tried to sexually assault her."

"Oh, my God. Noah, that's terrible." He could hear the terror in Rylee's voice. If anyone had done that to his baby sister, Noah would have ripped them to shreds. He hadn't wanted to restrain Lucas when he'd attacked Eli. He'd wanted the bastard to get exactly what he deserved, but he also didn't want Lucas to get arrested for battery and assault, because Eli struck him as a vengeful person who would try to do just that.

"Rylee, since we arrived back here, it's been a hot mess. Kenya confronted Eli, and at first he tried to deny it, but when pushed, he finally cracked and admitted everything."

"So what's next?"

"Not sure yet, but I have a feeling good ole' Eli will

get what he has coming, especially if his partner and former best friend Lucas has anything to say about it."

"And you? What about you and Chynna? I take it you didn't propose?"

Noah glanced at the doorway to make sure Chynna hadn't moved and couldn't hear him. "Hell no! How could I?" He whispered into the phone. "She had the concert and then we came back to the hotel and the next morning we learned of Kenya's attack. The timing has been all wrong."

"I understand," Rylee said. "But the timing is never going to be right, Noah. Somehow you're going to have to carve some time out for you two. Make your relationship a priority."

"And I will," Noah said, "when all this settles down."

"Alright, give Chynna my love, and I can't wait to see you, big bro. Love you."

"And I love you. See you soon." Noah ended the call. He stared at Chynna's back. Rylee was right somehow, someway. He had to find the right moment to get down on one knee and make Chynna his forever.

CHAPTER 15

*T*he press surrounding Kenya's attack was constant for Lucas and Kenya, but it was nothing short of routine compared to the press coverage that exploded after Eli's arrest several days later. The police had gotten the thug to confess to Eli's involvement in the scheme to attack Kenya, and Eli had been arrested. Unfortunately, he'd made bail, but Lucas had warned him that if he stepped foot in the R&K Records' office, he would regret it. Not that life was faring well on that front either.

The R&K Records' office had been besieged by the press. They all wanted to know if Lucas had any idea of Eli's machinations. *Had Eli really been that jealous of Lucas and Kenya's relationship?* They asked. Lucas had hired bodyguards for himself just to get to the office and his penthouse every day. Worse yet, he was trying to find a loophole that would allow him to dissolve his and Eli's partnership and still keep R&K Records afloat. Several advertisers for his artists wanted to pull their endorsements given the bad publicity R&K was receiving. It was a PR nightmare.

The only thing good in Lucas's life was Kenya. Outwardly, she was starting to heal from her attack, but he knew deep down she would hold scars, might always have them. He just hoped that he would be able to get her past them so they could move on to their future together.

He was thinking about what their future would hold when Kenya walked through his office later that afternoon. Most of her bruises had been covered with makeup, and she looked as beautiful as ever. She wore a cranberry keyhole halter silk dress that stopped just above her knee and showed off her athletic legs.

"Hey, you," she said, smiling warmly at him. "I was hoping to steal you away for dinner."

Lucas glanced down at his watch. It was nearly six pm. He'd been working so hard, he'd forgotten. His stomach growled in response, reminding him he hadn't eaten all day because he'd been so caught up in doing damage control.

"Dinner sounds great." Lucas shut his laptop and rose from his executive chair to walk over and brush his lips across hers. "Let's get out of here."

KENYA LEFT Lucas in ignorance to their destination and just directed him over to the Perch where, thanks to Chynna's influence, she'd secured their rooftop lounge exclusively for the night for her and Lucas's dinner. She hadn't allowed Lucas to change and had told him his black silk shirt and trousers would suit their surroundings just fine.

"Where are we going," Lucas asked as he stepped out of the car. He wasn't familiar with the old Art Deco building.

"You'll see," Kenya said, taking his hand and leading him to the elevator.

After they arrived on the sixteenth floor, they were greeted by French inspired antique furniture that reminded Kenya of the bohemian French bistros she'd visited during the summer she'd gone to Paris with a friend from NYU. The outside was even more impressive, with plush couches, firepits and lush landscaping. The host led them to a private table that gave them a three-hundred-and-sixty degree view of downtown Los Angeles.

"How did I do?" Kenya asked, looking at Lucas as he glanced around the tropical terrace.

"Wonderful," Lucas said, smiling. This was exactly what he needed to let go of all the drama of the last week.

"Good, because we're going to enjoy some great food. I heard Chef Justin's food is some of the best."

And it was. They shared a bottle of champagne and enjoyed delicious tuna tartare, seafood bouillabaisse and pork belly for dinner before finishing with crème brûlée for Lucas and a chocolate pot de crème that Kenya dove into.

"Can I tell you how much I needed this," Lucas said, wiping his mouth with his napkin after the crème brûlée.

"I know this week has been difficult for you." Kenya stared at him intently. She could see the worry lines around his eyes with trying to keep R&K Records afloat.

"For me?" Lucas said. "It's nothing, just speculation, but you? You're the one who was hurt in all this. You're the victim here."

"I'm no one's victim," Kenya stated firmly. "We," she said, pointing to him, "are going to get through this because we have each other. I will not let Eli take our power away from us."

"That's what I've always loved about you, Kenya," Lucas eyes shone brightly when he looked at her. "Your spirit, your fire."

Kenya smiled. "Good, because I'm burning up now, and I have a fire that needs to be quenched."

Lucas's brow rose slightly. She hoped he'd get her bold assertion. Since they'd both declared their love for each other, Lucas had been walking on eggshells about even touching her and would only wrap his arms around her every night. She was tired of being treated like she was a delicate piece of glass and was going to break. She knew he was just being respectful since the attack, but she wanted him to make love to her, and she'd orchestrated tonight's romantic dinner to ensure that happened.

Kenya rose from the wrought-iron chair and held her hand out to him. Without words, she told him that she wasn't afraid and wanted to be close again as close as two people could get. Lucas accepted her hand, and together they walked off the balcony.

Once they made it back to Lucas's, the passion they'd been holding inside for days was set loose, and it was just as hot as it had been that first night they were together. Except this time, Lucas was more gentle and soft. This time, he lifted her off her feet and carried her to the bedroom. He gently laid her atop his damask comforter and slowly, tenderly unzipped the color-block sheath she'd been wearing and slid it from her body until she was wearing nothing but lacy undies.

As he undressed, removing his jacket, then unbuttoning his shirt, Kenya watched him unabashedly as the shirt fell to the floor. She feasted her eyes on his chiseled abs. He was so sexy and he was hers, all hers. She slid off the bed to stand in front of Lucas to help him with the buckle of his trousers. He kissed her neck and shoulders as she released the buckle and unzipped his pants. They fell to the floor in a bundle at his feet, and he stepped out of them and then spun her around so her back was to his front, and he could remove the lace bra she wore. It fell to her feet just as he cupped and molded her breasts with his hands.

The feelings were so delicious; she couldn't help moaning and leaning her head back against his shoulder. She felt his erection against her backside and reached inside his shorts to caress his hard package. Lucas groaned, but he didn't stop. Instead, he continued massaging her breasts and roaming his hands down the side of her body until he came to her hips. He began sliding her lace cheeky panties down and they too met their matching partner on the floor. Kenya tensed slightly when she felt his fingers teasing the folds of her womanhood so he could slide inside, but she wasn't tense for long. Lucas stroked her in and out, in and out until she trembled with need. She couldn't focus on him anymore; all she could do was wrap her arms around the back of his neck as he brought her to ecstasy.

"God, Kenya, I need you," he murmured against the damp skin of her chin against his jaw.

"Then take me," she moaned. "Take me."

Lucas leaned Kenya over the bed and with her butt high in the air, he took her from behind. He thrust inside her, and Kenya moaned. He thrust again, and Kenya thought she would die from pleasure. Lucas lowered himself until his chest was against her back, and he could reach around her to stroke her breasts with one hand while he thrust inside her. The penetration was so deep, she surrendered herself to it.

"Oh, sweet Jesus," he groaned, stroking her hair, back and butt. Then he slid his fingers to her womanhood so he could fondle her clitoris while he thrust inside her. Kenya reached an orgasm quickly and cried out, "Lucas!"

She was barely over her first orgasm when Lucas changed position and perched on the edge of the bed and made her sit on top of his still-hard erection. Kenya gripped his shoulders firmly and gyrated her pelvis vigorously to meet the strong sensations caused by Lucas rocking his hips backward and forward. His thrusts were simultaneous with her motions, and Kenya's head began to toss from side to side and a second orgasm overtook her.

And this time Lucas was not far behind, because he thrust one final time, and he too groaned, clutching her to his chest. Her hair fell across his sweaty face, and Lucas brushed it aside to look up at her. "I love you."

"And I love you."

CHYNNA WASN'T happy that Noah had to leave to go back to Tucson a couple of days after Kenya's attack. He had to get back to the ranch because of an emergency. Apparently, Caleb had fallen during a bull ride and was hospitalized. It was exactly what they didn't need. It seemed like they were always dealing with one crisis after another. *Will we ever have a break?*

Thankfully, Chynna had her tour to keep her occupied, but that hadn't stopped the press from following her. They all wanted to know what was next for her after Eli's arrest for orchestrating Kenya's attack. They wanted to know how she felt. Did she feel responsible? Was she going to stay at R&K Records? Was she going to continue seeing Noah Hart?

Questions. Questions. Chynna stared into the dressing mirror in St. Louis. Sometimes she wished she could crawl under a rock and get away from it all.

That's when she remembered that she *did* have another home—a home where she could be herself and no one judged her.

Chynna picked up her cell and made a few phone calls and before long, travel arrangements had been made. She was already dressed in jeans and a T-shirt when Deacon stopped into her dressing room to tell her the limo was waiting to take her back to the hotel.

"Deacon, how many days until our next tour stop?"

"Three. Why?" he asked, looking at her suspiciously.

Chynna smiled. "Good because I'm leaving." When Deacon frowned, she clarified. "I'm not going to run away and send Kenya back in my place, if that's what you're thinking."

Deacon laughed. "Well, that is kind of played out now."

"Yes, but I am going to take two days off." Chynna reached for her purse, swung it over her shoulder and headed toward the door.

"And go where?"

Chynna turned back around long enough to say, "Now what fun would that be if I told you?" She smiled. "But I promise I will be back. And this time I will be accessible by phone."

NOAH URGED the cows forward with his stallion toward the pasture. He hadn't wanted to come back home. He'd wanted to stay in Los Angeles with Chynna. But family had beckoned. His knucklehead brother, Caleb, who was supposed to be holding down the fort, had decided to have some fun at a nearby rodeo and had fallen off a bull. Caleb now had broken ribs and a concussion to show for his efforts. He wouldn't be able to keep his eye on the ranch while he recovered, which meant that Noah had to get home and take care of business.

Chynna had said she was okay with his leaving, but Noah felt like such a heel leaving her only days after her entire world had been rocked by learning that the scum who owned part of her record label had tried to hurt Kenya. Noah planned on getting back to LA as soon as he could. He'd already talked to his father about hiring a second-in-command that could take care of the ranch in his absence.

He wasn't about to retire and traipse with Chynna around the world, but he also intended for their marriage to be a full one which would require him to be able to leave on occasion to meet her while she was on the road. Speaking of marriage, in the couple of days he'd had before he'd left, he hadn't been able to ask Chynna to marry him. The moment hadn't been right, but one day soon it would be. And when it was, he wouldn't waste another second.

He was disembarking and had tied up Max to take a break under a tree when he saw a horse galloping toward him in the distance. With the sun so high overhead, Noah couldn't get a good look at who it was until she was nearly in front of him. Chynna.

She smiled broadly when she reached him. "Hey, cowboy."

"Hey, yourself," Noah said, looking up at her. "What are you doing here? Shouldn't you be on tour?"

"I'm still on tour. I just decided to come here for a couple of days. Do you have a problem with that?"

"Not a chance," Noah said as he reached for her and helped her down from her favorite palomino. He lowered his head and kissed her deeply.

She met his urgent kiss with the same intensity, and they sunk into the grass. They were greedy for each other and their mouths fused, tongues mingled—it was earthy, sensual and hot. Heat and awareness were everywhere. Chynna's arms tightened around Noah's neck, and he couldn't help letting his palms skim the curve of her breast. Chynna tilted her hips upward and she collided with his burgeoning erection. Noah growled low in his throat.

He couldn't just romp in the grass with the woman that would be his wife, at least not yet, not until he made her his officially. Slowly, he grabbed one of her arms and pulled her up until they were both in the seated position.

Chynna's eyes were glazed with passion, and she couldn't understand why Noah had stopped. "What's wrong?" she asked. "I thought that was pretty hot." She'd been ready to have her first romp in the hay—or in this case, grass—with her cowboy.

"Nothing," Noah said, inhaling deeply. "I just think now is the time." He'd been waiting for the "right moment," but like Rylee had said, would there ever be a right moment? He just had to go for it.

"Time for what?"

Noah rose ever-so slightly until he was on bended knee with the other on the ground.

"Noah," Chynna's eyes grew large. He wasn't sure if it was fear or excitement, but he was going for it.

"Chynna," Noah reached for her right hand. "I know this may seem sudden, but I'm one of those people that believe that when you know, *you know*. And I know that I love you with all my heart, and there's not another woman for me on this earth. You're the woman for me, so would you do me the honor of becoming my wife? Would you marry me?"

Chynna stared at Noah in disbelief, not because he loved her and wanted to marry her, but because like him, she knew unequivocally that she could spend the rest of her life with him. Getting lost and having her Jeep crash into the Golden Oaks Ranch had been one of the best things that had ever happened to her. It had changed the course of her life and, as a result, she'd found a place she could call home.

"Yes, I will marry you, Noah Hart."

Noah's eyes teared up. "You will?"

"Yes, yes, I will marry you,"

Noah hollered and gave a "Woohoo!" and swept her into his arms, kissing her fervently. "I'm sorry I don't have the ring right now. It's back up at the house."

"I don't care about a ring," Chynna cried through happy tears. "I only want you."

"And I want you."

EPILOGUE

"*K*enya, Kenya, over here," Several photographers called out her name as she and Lucas walked the red-carpet at the Oscars the following year.

"Go ahead, babe," Lucas beamed at her in his Giorgio Armani tuxedo. "It's your night to shine."

Kenya smiled at him before walking over to the legions of photographers camped out on the red carpet. She was still amazed by all the light and cameras as they snapped pictures on her in her one of a kind red strapless Marchesa gown. She couldn't believe after the roller-coaster year she'd had that *she* was in the spotlight. Carter Wright's film had been nominated for an Oscar and Kenya had been nominated for Best Actress for her role as Yvette.

One of the reporters from an entertainment show came over to her on the red-carpet, "How does it feel to be considered a shoe-in for the Best Actress win?" The woman asked.

"Oh, I don't know about that, I'm against some tough competition. It's really an honor just to be nominated."

"It's been a crazy year for you what with imitating your sister, a famous singer and all. How have you coped with the instant stardom?"

Kenya gave her a sidewards glance, "I don't let the fame get to me because at the end of the day, it's really about knowing who you are and being comfortable in your own skin. I'm not just an actress, but a sister and..." she glanced at Lucas, "A soon to be wife." She held up her hand that held a large engagement ring.

"Congratulations!" The woman gushed, holding her hand. "That's quite a rock. Looks like R&K Records is booming despite the dissolution of your husband's partnership."

"Thank you." Kenya nodded. She'd been worried herself, but Lucas had rallied and thanks to a clause in the partnership agreement had been able to dissolve Eli's involvement, but retain ownership of the name. R&K Records had stayed afloat and was now back on the rise with Chynna's fourth album. It was a departure from her second and third album, but Kenya was happy to see her sister finally making music she loved.

Speaking of which, Kenya's eye caught Chynna coming up the red carpet with her husband, Noah Hart. He too was wearing a tuxedo which although not his style, he looked dapper.

The reporter followed Kenya's gaze and saw Chynna coming up the walkway. She rushed toward her, yelling at her cameraman to follow. "We have to get a picture of the two of you together."

"Absolutely!" Kenya replied, grabbing the train of her dress and following the reporter.

"Chynna," she motioned her sister over, "C'mon over."

Chynna smiled broadly as she walked toward them. She looked ever the diva in a silver studded floor-length-gown with a racerback neckline that hugged every one of her sister's God-given curves. Chynna leaned over and gave Kenya a quick peck on the cheek as to not ruin her make-up.

"DOESN'T MY SISTER LOOK GREAT!" Chynna gushed as she smiled at the reporter. She knew the reporter want to talk about her and her new album, but she wanted tonight to be about Kenya and not about her. Tonight, she needed to take a backseat.

"She sure does," The reporter responded. "But so do you, you are rocking that dress, girlfriend."

Chynna laughed. "Thank you."

"Is it hard for you seeing Kenya in the role of Yvette which was once yours?"

Although not visible to others, Chynna could see Kenya tense slightly at her side at reporter's bold question, but it would be one that everyone would be thinking and was too afraid to ask. Chynna was surprised the reporter had the balls to ask, but it was Hollywood after all.

"Absolutely not." Chynna reached over and grasped Kenya's delicate hand in hers and gave a gentle squeeze of encouragement. "This role was made for sister and I have every confidence that she's going to take that gold statuette home tonight. My husband and I," she motioned Noah and Lucas over to them. "Will be rooting for her."

"Thank you, twinie," Kenya mouthed.

Chynna mouthed back. "You're welcome."

The two men in their lives walked over and Noah slid his arm around Chynna's waist and Lucas did the same to Kenya.

When the reporter realized she wouldn't get a rise

out of Chynna or Kenya, she said, "You all are mighty fine looking couples. Enjoy the rest of tonight." After a quick picture, she and her cameraman rushed off to find another celebrity.

"Thank you," Chynna and Kenya said in unison like two halves of the same whole.

BOOKS BY YAHRAH ST. JOHN

Connected Books
One Magic Moment
Dare to Love

Dirty Laundry Series
Dirty Laundry
Can't Get Enough

Stand Alone Novels
Never Say Never
Risky Business of Love

Hart Series
Entangled Hearts
Entangled Hearts 2
Untamed Hearts
Restless Hearts
Unchained Hearts
Chasing Hearts Pub Date
Captivated Hearts

Mitchell Brother Series
Claimed by the Hero
Seducing the Seal

Coming Soon in 2022
Guarding His Princess

ABOUT THE AUTHOR

Yahrah St. John became a writer at the age of twelve when she wrote her first novella after secretly reading a Harlequin romance. Throughout her teens, she penned a total of twenty novellas. Her love of the craft continued into adulthood. She's the proud author of thirty-nine books with Harlequin Desire, Kimani Romance and Arabesque as well as her own indie works.

When she's not at home crafting one of her spicy romances with compelling heroes and feisty heroines with a dash of family drama, she is gourmet cooking or traveling the globe seeking out her next adventure. For more info: www.yahrahstjohn.com or find her on Facebook, Instagram, Twitter, Bookbub or Goodreads.